Challenging The Deveon Warrior

Deveon & Anhelios Saga
Book Two
Jennifer Marcia

Challenging The Deveon Warrior
Deveons & Anhelios Saga
Book Two

With humanity on the brink of an apocalypse, there is no time to spare. The Deveons, six fallen angels destined to save mankind, must fight the Anhelios and the gods themselves to save not only one another and the whole of humanity, but their fated mates.

Nikki St. James has always been a little more than most people know how to handle. She is loud, opinionated, and aggressive. She is also a Chosen One. A human Hunter destined to fight the Anhelios to help save humanity. She may also be one of the Fallen, a Deveon Warrior forced to reincarnate in human form after trying to save humanity. If she is, she could very well be Azrael Dennison's true mate.

Azrael has spent millennia following his chosen brothers in their quest for the Deveon Queen. Now that they have found her, his mate may be within arm's length until the gods themselves rip her from this dimension in a twisted game of chess to see who has the skills necessary to complete their bonds.

Challenging the Deveon Warrior is a spicy 18+ Dark Paranormal Romance. Content warnings for this book include: spicy sex on page, some bondage, BDSM aspects, violence, gore, language, religious concepts, and dark themes. Please be gentle with yourselves and check my website for more content information.

Chapter One

M oving On

Four years ago

Nikki

I packed my duffel bag quickly. This wasn't my first time packing my bags to leave the place I reluctantly called home. I didn't really want to think about the number of times I had done this shit over the years. I inwardly groaned as I threw my jeans, T-shirts, and hooded sweatshirts into my bag along with my workout leggings and sports bras.

I actually hated the part where I had to leave a foster home or group home or wherever it was I had managed to land in this time. I hated it almost as much as I hated moving onto the next one. The happy family pretense, when we all knew most of them didn't actually give a shit and were just after the additional paycheck that came with a new foster kid.

The group homes were at least honest about the transactional aspect of the system. They provided a dorm-type situation and classes, and we participated and didn't try to run away so they got to keep the government checks. I'm not saying no one cared about us. At some point they probably did, but the system was bent at best, and we were all just treading water and trying to keep our heads up.

I was done with this shit though. I was eighteen tonight and officially an adult. I had just aged out of my current group home, and no one cared if I walked out those doors. I was hell bent on getting out of here.

"Nikki." I heard my name from the doorway and looked over to see the administrator of Magnolia House standing in the girls' dorm doorway.

"Agnus." I replied.

"You don't have to leave tonight, Nichole. You can stay for a while longer. It's safe here." The woman who had dictated my day to day for the last two years told me softly as she watched me drop my ass on the twin bed and slip on my Converse sneakers.

She stood in the doorway, concern etched across her pretty features. "Thanks Agnus. I appreciate that. Honestly, and no offense, you have been kind to me, but my birthday feels like an early release, and I'm taking that shit and running with it." I smiled at the woman as I wiped my hands on my jeans and got up to empty my nightstand of the few items I called my own.

I slipped my cell phone into my pocket and a couple of books into the duffle bag. I plucked a blue file from the drawer and placed it into the bag. I didn't have to look to know it contained my birth certificate, social security card, and the last known address for the woman who had given me up at birth. She had died of a drug overdose when I was just a few years old so I knew there weren't any answers there, but I felt an intense pull toward the town on the birth certificate: Devil's Bend, Arizona. A few months ago I had received a letter from a lawyer there with the directive to come by or call after my eighteenth birthday. The letter mentioned an inheritance, but I was skeptical.

Somehow I had ended up in Phoenix about three hours away from the town that had been my mother's home. I had never been there, but the fifty dollars in my pocket was enough for a bus ticket and a hot meal, and I had every intention of using it for exactly that.

I returned my attention to Agnus and smiled. "I have plans, Agnus. Don't worry about me. I got my high school equivalency. Some money in my pocket. I'm good." The bitterness came through in my voice as I tried to move past her.

"Nikki," she said quietly, her hand on my forearm just over the new tattoo Brandon Ross had given me as a birthday gift. It was a she-devil emerging from flames. It took up a good portion of my inner arm and was absolutely badass. She raised her brow but said nothing about it as she pulled me into a tight hug. "Take care of yourself, Nik. I am so proud of you. You are an exceptional young woman, and I have no doubt you are going places in this life." She smiled a watery smile as she reluctantly released me and placed a wad of bills in my hand.

I blinked back tears as I stared at her, and Agnus Phillips' smile grew wider. "You didn't think I'd let you leave without a birthday gift did you?" she asked softly, and I hugged her again, a slight tremble in my arms as I held on tight. I was good at the tough girl act, but I was still just a kid, and I would be lying if I didn't admit, even if it was just to myself, how absolutely terrified I actually was. "You can stay, Nik. Go to community college. Work here as a counselor for room and board. You don't always have to take the hard road," she told me as the tears slipped past my lashes.

I shook my head. "Thank you, Ms. Phillips. I appreciate that so much. And part of me would like that, but I think I really do have to go. I think the hard road may just be my destiny." The words surprised me even as I said them, but they felt true, and I left it at that as I straightened and wiped my eyes.

Angus nodded and smiled tightly. "We all have to choose our own paths, Ms. St. James. I just hope you choose the right one for you. And know that you can always find a home here, Nik"

I nodded. "Thanks," I said softly as I headed for the door. I left Ms. Phillips in the dorm room and headed down the hall.

I wasn't what you would call a well-adjusted woman, teenager, whatever. I was angry and sometimes violent. Life hadn't been kind to me when I was smaller and weaker. I had no intention of ever being a victim again. With that knowledge came a tough exterior and an anger problem. I had been working on it in mandatory therapy, but really that just translated into picking up an aptitude for fighting and bad behavior.

It had served me well so far. I had always been somewhat difficult, and I didn't exactly plan on changing anytime soon. Still, that was then, and now, in this moment, I was ready to see what the universe had in store for me. I was excited and so naive. Little did I know that nothing in this world was as it seemed. I was about to step into a reality so vastly different from what I had once known that the two realities didn't even resemble one another.

Chapter Two

Devils Bend
Three years later
Nikki

My music is much too loud, a catchy tune about being vanilla in a world of hand necklaces and spankings. I dance around my yellow kitchen in too short booty shorts and a tight tank top, most likely annoying my neighbors but honestly not giving a shit. The knock on my door was expected as I turn down the music and head for the door. I flip open the latch to find a gorgeous blond girl about my age standing on the front step of my apartment.

She smiles softly. "Nikki?"

I lift an eyebrow at her. "Yep." I step back to let her in. The woman slips past me into the living room and sets her bag on the couch.

"Brandon sent me. I'm Kate Swinson. Can I sit?" she asks politely.

I smile at her. "Suit yourself." I flop down on the chair across from the couch. "How can I help you, Kate?" I smile at the woman across from me.

"Brandon said you could help train me."

I nod. "I can. I work at the fight club on Fifteenth and Olive. I'm a cage fighter there. Are you looking to join the roster?" I look her over. She is shorter than me and has a solid base. If she is any good, she might be hard to take down in a fight.

Kate smiles. "No. I'm more interested in self-defense. Someone I know went missing. I'm looking into it, but it's getting sketchier than I originally thought."

I look her over. There had been quite a few girls our age missing in the area over the past few months. I'm beginning to suspect possible human trafficking. It appears this woman thought so too. I nod at Kate.

"Ok. I can definitely help. Are you thinking about taking on a group of sketchy guys by yourself?" I am somewhat impressed by her moxie.

"Something like that. The problem is I've been looking into this frat at the college in Forthaven. I feel like they are connected to this girl's disappearance. She swiped on a Tinder match with one of the fraternity brothers. Even told me that they were meeting up for coffee and then just disappeared. The guy swears she never showed up for the date. But ..."

"But you think he has something to do with it," I say softly.

"Yes." Kate nods at me. "I just have this gut feeling that something is very wrong there. I'm not paranoid. I usually go with the flow, but these guys freaked me the fuck out. Like hair standing up all over my body freaked out. And, yesterday I saw one of them outside my apartment. I really don't want to go back there. I'm seriously considering getting a hotel."

I nod. "So you live in the area?"

Kate nods. "Yeah, the missing girl was my roommate. I'm pretty sure those assholes know I'm suspicious of them, and now they know where I live." Kate shudders.

"Not anymore. You can stay with me while we figure this out."

Kate looks at me, surprised. "You don't even know me. I could be a serial killer."

I laugh. "Trust me when I say, you are definitely not the serial killer in this scenario."

She smiles. " I appreciate it, but I can't afford to pay rent on two places," Kate says, worrying her lip between her teeth.

I smile back at her. "Honestly, it's fine. No rent necessary. My grandmother left me this apartment when she passed away so it's not a hardship."

Kate lets out a sigh and nods tightly. "Ok. Thank you, Nikki."

"Now we just gotta get you trained before anyone else disappears," I say, having no idea just how little time we have before the next disappearance.

· · · ·

"It's been two months since I met Kate, but it feels like we've known each other forever. We train everyday and deep dive into the sketchy fraternity daily. We're close to something, I can feel it,"I tell my friend Brandon, the manager of the gym I work at, as I watch Kate spar with a new cage fighter.

Brandon nods. He stands next to me, shoulder to shoulder, as we watch the girls. "I'm worried about you Nikki," he says seriously.

I scoff. "Bullshit. I'm the most bad ass woman you know. Not a chance you're worried." I say light heartedly as I knock his shoulder with mine.

Brandon side-eyes me. "This is true. And yet the guys you're looking into could be seriously bad people, Nik. I don't like it."

I turn to look at my friend. "This is what I was made for, Brandon. I can feel it. I'm not a nice girl. I'm not looking for love and cookies and puppy dog kisses. I'm a fighter, and I look out for the underdog. These missing women are the fucking underdog, and I'll be damned if I sit on my incredibly toned ass and do nothing to stop these assholes while the women just slip away."

Brandon nods tightly. "It is a nice ass," he ponders without looking at said ass.

I smile. "I know, right?".

He laughs. "Just be careful, Nik. I don't want you to go missing while you're busy trying to save everyone else."

I nod. "That's fair."

Several hours later, Kate and I finish our workout. Brandon and the others left hours ago. It's late, and we close up the gym. I live a few blocks from work and tend to walk. Tonight is no different, and Kate and I head out the back door of the gym and down the alley like any other night.

It's quiet. Too quiet, I think as the silence stretches and the hairs on the back of my neck stand on end. I place my hand on Kate's arm to stop her just as a figure steps out of the shadows in front of us. He smiles. It is not a friendly smile. Kate makes a low growling sound in the back of her throat just before she lunges at him. He throws a punch to her midsection, and she doubles over in pain.

I move into a fighter's crouch and circle the man as Kate catches her breath. I wait until he moves closer to me, and as his face comes out of the shadows, I register that this is the frat brother who Kate believes lied about meeting her roommate just before she disappeared. I kick out a leg and side swipe him. He goes down hard on both knees. I hear the crunch as his knees hit the pavement in the dark alley.

"You will regret that," a voice says from behind as strong arms lift me. My body tightens in response as I am lifted off my feet. The restraint feels surreal. I hadn't heard footsteps or felt a presence behind me. It shouldn't have been possible for anyone to get this close without my instincts kicking in. I am trained to sense any change in the environment around me.

A slow clap comes from the shadows of the alley, and my head snaps in the direction of the sound. A man steps out of the shadows. He is tall. Much taller than average with wavy blond curls and brilliant blue eyes. He appears to be in his late twenties, possible early thirties, with a strong jaw and broad shoulders. His face is twisted into a cruel smile.

"So this is the annoying human that has been poking around in our business," the man says with an annoyed tone of voice.

The man holding me sniffs my neck, and I shudder with repulsion. "It smells human," he states, his tone bored.

The tall man nods. "It probably is nothing more than a troublesome human girl biting off more than it can swallow," he says as he circles me.

"Michael. I appreciate your help, but I can handle them just fine," the frat brother says as he regains his feet and brushes the dirt from his expensive clothing.

The one holding me snorts. I remember I am captive and begin to struggle and fight against the unnatural strength of him as he holds me.

"No, Stan. It doesn't appear as if you can," the man called Michael says without emotion as he continues to observe me kicking and fighting against my captor.

I feel Kate begin to inch away from all of us, and I send her a silent plea to run as fast as she can. I hope she gets away because this situation is quickly getting out of control.

Michael smiles as he observes my attempts to get away. "This one may be something more than human, brother. She appears strong. She doesn't cower in fear as she should."

My blood feels cold beneath my skin at his words, and my heart seizes. I feel true terror as I watch him. I haven't had an easy life, and I have been exposed to bad people before, but something in my gut tells me I have never known evil like the man who watches me.

He smiles. "There it is. This one is finally appropriately terrified." He sniffs the air. "Delicious."

I shudder again, and the one holding me laughs. "I like it, Michael. Can I keep it?" he says close to my ear. I kick backwards at him and attempt to headbutt him. The laughter is mocking as his hold on me increases to the point of pain.

Michael shakes his head. "Gabriel, contain the girl. She is not a toy. Stan, please restrain the other one. She is further away than I find comfortable."

The frat brother, Stan, shoots down the alley toward Kate, and my heart drops. I feel nauseous as it occurs to me that Micheal never even turned his head to observe Kate as she slipped away from us. So either he was aware of her and allowed her to slip further away as a way of toying with us, or he was hyper aware of his surroundings, much like me. Either scenario would make our eventual escape more difficult.

Michael watches me as I work all of this out, and his smile turns feral. "We will take them. I am interested to see what they are. If they are simply human, then we can use them for their intended purpose. But if they are something more ..." Michael rubs his hands together as if he is almost gleeful. "... then I am excited to see what comes next. Perhaps we are close to exposing the missing Fallen."

With that, his appearance changes. His skin almost appears to glow, and a huge pair of white wings snaps out from his wide shoulders.

My head feels light as I watch Stan hand my new friend off to this strange winged being. I can hear the sound of wings unfurling behind me, and the man holding me suddenly takes flight. My consciousness begins to flow in and out as my body becomes weightless, and we are hurled through the air at an impossible speed. The ground is quickly fading away. We are so high up, and while I fight to stay conscious, the shock of what I have just witnessed and am currently experiencing is too much, and my eyes flutter closed.

Chapter Three

The Dungeon
Present Day
Nikki

I awake with a start. *Jesus, this shit is getting old.* I rub the pain in my shoulder from sleeping on the hard ground. We've been in this fucking dungeon from months now, and I'm tired, dirty, and incredibly frustrated. There is no way out. I watch as my only friend left in the world wakes up next to me.

"Fuck. Still here," she says in a whisper as if maybe this was all a dream and she was actually going to wake up in her bed at the apartment.

I snort. "Yep. Still here."

She opens her eyes to take in the dark room.

"What day is it?" She has asked the same question everyday since we arrived three months ago.

"Wednesday. I think day 88."

She nods stands, and begins stretching. I do the same.

"Ok. So they will be here soon to begin training and interrogation. Take whatever you can from the training. They are good. We'll need that if we're ever going to get out," I remind her.

Kate laughs bitterly. "Whatever these winged beasts are, some type of angels or demons, they are never going to let us go, Nik."

"They may never *let* us go, but eventually they are going to slip up, and we will get out of here. I can feel it."

Kate sighs. "I hope you're right because I'm not sure how much more training and brainwashing I can take before we end up drinking the kool-aid, girl. Three months and I'm hanging on by a thread."

I smile tightly at my friend. "We'll get out of here babe. I know it."

• • • • •

The door opens with a creak, and we are greeted with what has become our morning breakfast trays. Plastic cafeteria trays with plastic bowls of oatmeal. A cup of milk and a cup of water. There are packets of brown sugar and packaged butter tabs which, to be honest, make the food bearable. The trays also include a bowl of warm water and a rough washcloth to clean up with after our meal. I reach for my tray, and Kate laughs a little bitterly.

"Gods, do you remember when we first came here and refused to eat or drink anything for days?" she says as she reaches for her own tray.

I nod as I add the sugar and butter to my oatmeal. "We were worried they would drug us, but they just wanted to bore us to death," I reply as I eat my oatmeal.

Kate nods. "Bore us and drown us in mediocrity so that their version of reality is desirable to all of this," she says sharply as she waves a hand out at our current accommodations.

I place my bowl on the tray and reach out to hug Kate. "It's going to be ok, girl. We've got this."

She wipes the tears from her face and takes a sip of her water.

"I'm scared, Nik. I don't know how much longer I can do this before I give in. I don't want to join their damn army of angels. I know they can't be the 'good guys' if their version of good is stealing human women with an Anhelio or angel bloodline and forcing them to train to find and fight other Anhelios."

I nod. "I know. The Hunters appear to have increased strength and skills. We appear to have these skills. They need us for their army. They aren't going to hurt us."

Kate blinks slowly, "Any more than they already have?"

I tighten my arms around my friend.

"The Anhelios are determined to find and secure an army of archangels and hunters for some kind of coming war. As long as we keep learning and training, they won't hurt us," I tell her with more confidence than I feel.

I feel the shiver that goes through Kate before I release her. "They are bat-shit crazy and terrifying."

I nod and frown slightly. "They really are. The other captives are quickly slipping into warrior mode and becoming their army. We have to hold onto reality for as long as possible."

Kate nods and smiles at me just as Gabriel, the sadistic angel who had been my captor the night we were taken, kicks the door open and grunts at us. "Wash up, human whores. Stop talking before I show you what those mouths were actually meant to be used for."

I scowl at the disgusting beast who barks orders and sexual threats at us daily. I wash my face and hands with the warm water they provided and move past my friend to follow Gabriel to the restroom where I know I'll have five minutes to do my business before the next woman is sent in.

Next we are led to another room in the dungeon and guided through a series of exercises and routines until we are warmed up, then we are forced to fight one another. Gabriel stands at the edge of the mats and barks orders at us in an attempt to help us train. The fights teach us to anticipate our opponents skills and probable responses. It is educational, and we are undoubtedly better fighters than we had been three months ago.

After Gabriel's training sessions, another of the guards, Lutheran, a tall black man with dreads and soft brown eyes, comes to take us to our classes. The classes are taught in a room with heavy wooden tables and chairs and a blackboard where they go over their origin story and our purpose as humans and eventually Hunters. The classes are designed to essentially brainwash us into perceiving the world from their perspective and convince us to eventually join them. All of this, combined with the lack of stimulation and mundane nature of our days, is a magic formula for acceptance and acquiescence to their beliefs and ways. I am holding out though. We can see what they are doing and have been able to resist so far, but Kate is right, time is quickly running out.

• • • •

After dinner, Kate and I were pacing around our cell trying to work off the last of our energy when the door suddenly bursts open, and Gabriel stomps in.

"Move against the wall, human," Gabriel barks loudly as he forces me closer to the brick wall behind me. I hate to be chained to the wall. It makes me feel incredibly vulnerable, and honestly they haven't done it much lately. Perhaps they are spooked by something. If so, I hope we will be able to use it against them in the future.

"Fucking move!" Gabriel roars at me. I move to the wall and allow him to cuff me. "You too, little bitch." Gabriel barks at Kate. She steps up to the wall, and he cuffs her wrist to the metal bracelets attached there.

I stare at my friend in horror when another woman is brought in and thrown to the ground. The woman is gorgeous with huge dark brown eyes and long chestnut brown hair that falls down her back in waves. She is dressed in leggings and a white tank top that now has dirt streaks across the front. She rolls to her side in a defensive move that demonstrates her knowledge of self-defense.

Gabriel looks at her with disgust. "Useless human women. Only good for one thing." He leers at us and licks his lips while adjusting his pants.

I swallow back the bile from his insinuations and close my eyes. I hear the door slam, knowing that Gabriel has finally left.

The new woman smiles tightly as she scoots back against the wall and looks us over. There is something powerful about her, an intensity I've never experienced before, and my soul seems to acknowledge her as family. I've never actually had a real family before so the feeling is foreign and uncomfortable, and yet the rightness of it presses down on me. I rub my chest absently as I watch her. She looks horrified, and I can absolutely relate.

"You're new," Kate says simply, and the woman nods as she stands and adjusts her clothing.

"Yes."

I snort. "Gabriel didn't chain you." I'm suspicious by nature, and I'm not sure why they would chain us up and leave her.

The new girl nods. "I guess he doesn't see me as much of a threat."

I laugh, "Right. Or he just plans on dealing with you later." It's a cruel thing to say, but I am looking for her reaction. She doesn't disappoint when a shiver runs through her, and her face loses all color.

Kate glares at me. "Dammit, Nikki," she says forcefully as she turns to look at the horror etched across the woman's face. "Honestly, it's not like that. They don't hurt us like that. Gabriel just likes to insinuate that shit as a kind of psychological warfare. I'm Kate," Kate tells her, easing her discomfort.

I feel badly for having caused her distress. It was unkind, but in my own defense, I am in survival mode.

The new girl releases a breath and smiles tightly. "Fuck. Thank God. Ok. I wish I could say it's nice to meet you Kate, but I think we can all acknowledge that this shit is not looking good for any of us."

Seriously. She has a pretty strong grasp on the situation for a newbie. I don't know who this woman is, but I have an uncanny feeling that meeting her is going to change the trajectory of my life. I had no idea at the time just how right I was about that.

Chapter Four

N yx?
Azrael

The Queen is missing. Or rather, the human woman who is the embodiment of our Deveon Queen, the one the Anhelios refer to as the Queen of the Damned. The Fallen Angel who had been our leader and savior and who Isiah had finally found again in this lifetime.

Aliyah. Our leader and my chosen brother's fated mate. That woman is missing.

One minute she had been at the Deveon compound, training and learning, and then without warning, she had simply disappeared. Fuck. She had been doing fine so far. She seemed to accept Isiah, even be drawn to him. Even with his less desirable qualities, she is his mate and our leader, and something inside of her had seemed accepting of that. She is powerful and intelligent.

We need her. Isaiah needs her. Fuck, the world and especially the humans need her. We are running out of time, and now she is missing …again.

Good gods, this is a clusterfuck. I am currently going through the surveillance camera footage to see where she went. Rafa is pacing, and Isaiah is growling and destroying our house in his frustration over losing her.

"I got something!" I yell to my brothers as I zoom in on Aliyah as she exits my brother's bedroom window, drops to the tile roof below, and then swings down to the next level. We watch in awe as she drops twenty feet to the pool deck below my balcony and then turns to run into the desert.

"You've got to be fucking kidding me," Rafa says under his breath, and Isaiah just stares at the video in wonder.

"Ok. Fuck. We've got to find her. She could be anywhere by now," Isaiah says as he slams his hands down on the monitor table.

"Sure. If she had a vehicle. She doesn't, which means she's on foot. She can't be any further than Peyton Springs by now," I tell them both.

"Are you sure about that, motherfucker?" Isaiah asks, turning his frustration on me.

Rafa pans the cameras to the garage and does a quick sweep. "Yep. She's on foot."

"Right, but as soon as she hits town, she'll find herself a ride, and then she'll be in the damn wind again." Isaiah groans as he slams his hands down on the desk in front of me.

"Ok. We can't let that happen. Let's go grab our girl," Rafa says.

"*My* fucking girl," Isaiah growls at him.

I'm about to jump between the two of them before Isaiah puts hands on Rafa when a powerful Deveon vision cuts through our bullshit. Like a movie projecting in my mind's eye, we can see another's personal experiences should they be projected to the others in our bond.

It's Aliyah, and she's terrified. She is surrounded by Anhelios. Gabriel is holding her arms behind her back, and Michael has his claws pressing into her breast. I can smell the copper scent of her blood and feel her fear as clearly as if it is my own. The vision fades as they take flight with her.

"I'm going to remove both their motherfucking heads from their shoulders," Isaiah growls as he slams out of the surveillance room.

Isaiah heads to the weapons closet, Rafa disappears down the hall, and I head for the garage to grab the Escalade. We're all terrified for Aliyah. If the Anhelios know who she is, then getting her back isn't going to be easy.

Aliyah is the Chosen One. The only being who can unite the Fallen and unlock the memories of the others. Our mates.

Before the War of The Winged Beasts, when we first came across the prophecy of the fated mates and the angelic bonds, we didn't know pain. Once we began the bonds, we understood the pull of destiny, the pain of existing without our other half. It was a consequence of increasing our powers through the bonds we now lived with pain every day we were without our fated mates. Even for those of us who had not begun the bonding process before the war.

Like Rafa and the Anhelios, they lived with the same longing and loss, yet without the knowledge of who or what could ease the discomfort. Keyra and Nyx have been lost to us for millenia. It's painful to exist without them, and possibly more painful not to know if they were our other halves or if there was an unknown entity who could fill that role. In a way, Isaiah and I were lucky in the sense that we knew who we needed to find, however difficult that proved to be.

The others were not so lucky. And while it was true that we could bond with any other Anhelio, it was not the same as true mates.

We have to get Aliyah back and unlock her Deveon form, or humanity will be lost forever. We are running out of time. The Anhelios are getting antsy, and with our mates within grasp, they are bound to increase their attempts at annihilating the human race.

• • • •

We're familiar with the Anhelios compound. It's a large house that the Anhelios use as a meeting place. Their compound sits at the end of a long road, deep in the desert, about two hours outside of Peyton Springs. We make it there in a little over an hour. We could have been faster had we flown, but the car allows us the ability to transport the weapons, surveillance equipment, and the obscene amount of cash that Rafa feels we might need if something were to go wrong.

We park the SUV at the end of the long driveway and wait. The house is lit up and active with people moving about and classical music playing. "It doesn't appear that they are expecting us," Rafa says, surprised.

I nod."So perhaps they don't actually know who they have then."

"So, what? They just grabbed a random woman?"

"Best guess, they think she's a Hunter," I respond quietly, and Isaiah nods.

"So, do we go in with the surveillance equipment and try to locate her?" Rafa asks into the silence of the car.

I shake my head and take a few deep breaths. "Let me try the energy location first. Maybe her connection to Isaiah is strong enough for the gifts to work."

My brothers nod, and I close my eyes, breathing in deeply through my nose and out through my mouth. I need to be centered and focused.

The process takes time. Patience is not a strong suit for the other Deveons. As if on cue, Isaiah growls out, "What the actual fuck are we waiting for?" in frustration as I try to reach out with my senses to locate our queen.

I close my eyes and breathe in deeply as I open my chakras in an attempt to find Alyiah's energy. This is a gift we obtained when Isaiah and Alyiah bonded a millennia ago. There are many advantages to the bonds, one of which is the innate ability to find one another when necessary. Of course, our telepathy and location gifts works best when we are in our Deveon forms, but Alyiah has yet to acknowledge Isaiah as her mate and complete the bonds. Sowe have to work with what we have.

I smile tightly at my brother's impatience as I reach out for her essence. I can feel her energy. "I got her," I say quietly as a dull, throbbing red pulse touches my energy.

"Thank fuck," Isaiah breaths out next to me.

"It seems to be coming from inside the. I'm going to train my own energy on the pulse of her location."

I try to blend my energy with hers to give her some peace. A sense of security until we can get inside to free her, as she tries to wrap her head around whatever horrors she is imagining in this place.

We sit in silence. I am untangling my energy from hers when Aliyah suddenly projects another vision.

This time, she is falling into a dark, cell-like room with two other women. Her knees are scratched, and her arms are bruised. She is scared. It's a bone deep fear, and I have the sudden, completely unfounded fear that they have violated her. She is projecting a level of vulnerability that screams sexual assault. Isaiah is projecting his own vision of slowly peeling their skin from their bodies.

"That's it, we're going in," Isaiah announces, unable to take this any longer.

Rafa and I nod quickly, and we exit the vehicle to move around to the ground floor of the structure. The three of us slip in through an open window on the ground floor and then proceed to move towards the middle of the compound, hoping to find a doorway leading down.

I had seen the direction of her thoughts in the last vision, and we finally find it. There is a grouping of corridors that lead to different areas of the house and a doorway leading down. I stay at the doorway to keep guard and take out anyone who comes our way, while Rafa and Isaiah navigate the large, dungeon-like space.

I close my eyes and collect powerful protection energy from my root chakra to send with my brothers.

I return to my breathing as I wait for them to locate Aliyah and return. I focus on sending more protection energy her way when I become aware of a powerful entity close to me. I slip out of my trance state, draw my sword, and move behind the wall across from the doorway.

Moments later, a being moves into the space in front of me. Hs is smaller than me most beings are but not by much. His shoulders are broad, and he is tall. The man is dressed in an expensive black suit and wears his blond hair slightly long on top and slicked back. It reminds me of the 1920's. I slip my sword out and in front of his neck as his body stiffens.

"Michael. I believe you stole something that belongs to us," I utter as he remains completely still. His shoulders drop slightly, and his nod is almost imperceptible.

"Ah, yes. So the girl is something more than a mere Hunter," he replies quietly. I can feel the malevolent energy as it permeates from his skin, and I have to repress the shudder as it makes its way up my spine. He has very bad intentions towards the woman who was once our leader.

"She is," I reply calmly as I nudge him through the doorway and down the stairs. I am unsure what I will find in the dungeon below, but I am certain that the threat I present to the leader of the Anhelios will be enough to protect us from their wrath. At least as long as it takes to leave this place with our queen.

We emerge in the corridor below, and I can hear my brothers speaking to our queen. I notice the door to one of the cells is open. My brothers have already been here and forced their way inside.

We stop outside. Gabriel lays on the hard cement floor with my brother's knife through his heart.

"Gabe must have said something particularly nasty," I tell Michael, and he laughs harshly.

"You will pay for removing my best soldier from my troops, Deveon."

We move closer to the open cell when we hear Isaiah speaking.

"Aliyah, we can't take every broken human home with us," he tells her before Rafa interrupts him.

"Whatever she needs, Isaiah. We offer penance."

Isaiah nods in response, but Alyiah shakes her head.

"No. It's not that. They're mine," she says simply.

My heart sizes in my chest, and my body goes numb. *They're hers?* The words bounce around my skull as I absorb the meaning. The women she is confined with must be our fated mates. The other Fallen Angels who were damned by the gods to an eternity of reincarnation in human form until we could free ourselves from our hell dimension and find them. Complete the bonds and release their true Deveon forms.

Michael begins a slow clap at their words. My sword to Michael's throat doesn't appear to deter him from his emotionless response to the situation.

"So it's true. The Queen of the Damned has been awakened," he says sarcastically. Isaiah holds Aliyah with one hand and reaches for his sword with the other.

Michael laughs. "As much as you would like to kill me, Demon, it simply cannot be done."

"That may be true, Angel, and yet I can slow you down." Isaiah swings his sword and drops Michael's head to the ground beside him.

The wall drips with blood as Isaiah holds Aliyah closer. I nod to my brothers as I wipe the blood from my skin. Rafa passes one of the women to me and carries the other as we move toward the stairs in unison. The women seem to be in shock and while clearly capable and possibly even fighters, if not Hunters themselves, we must move quickly. I look at the woman in my arms and smile reassuringly as we move down the hall and away from the cell.

"I can fucking walk. I'm not an invalid or a child," she says with a bitter edge to her voice.

"Yep." I squeeze her tighter and pick up the pace.

"Are you going to release me?"

"As soon as we're clear of the compound, princess," I tell her tightly, and she stiffens in my arms.

My skin prickles in awareness as the woman I hold pings me with an electric shock she doesn't seem to feel. My blood warms at her nearness, and my soul cries out in acceptance and acknowledgement of my other half. I look down at her and take in the long dark hair, the gold skin, and the almond shaped eyes.

She is breathtaking in this form. Different from the woman I knew and was beginning to love in our Anhelio forms. She is human, weak and fragile. Not the winged mythical creature she once was. She lacks the strength and power of our Anhelio form and the powerful darkness of our Deveon form. And yet she is beautiful, like this. Even covered in dirt and sweat from this gods forsaken dungeon, she is mesmerizing.

"Are they dead?" the woman I hold asks softly.

"Unfortunately, no. Anhelios are immortal. It will slow them down though, and the healing process is a bitch," Rafa tells her with a wink. I swallow back the jealousy of his easy flirtation with her. He doesn't realize she is my fated mate.

"He called you a demon," the other woman says, her voice tight with fear.

Isaiah turns and smiles at her, flashing sharp teeth and red eyes. Kate stifles a scream, and Aliyah stiffens in Isaiah's arms.

"Don't worry babe, we're only devils in the very best sense of the word," Rafa tells the woman with a wink.

I swallow my nerves and fear as I help navigate our way out of the lower dungeon.

"You're worried about us, darling, when those monsters had you and your friend chained to a wall?" I ask as we slip out the window we came through, "Might be time to rethink your concepts on Good and Evil," I tell them as we run through the dark.

I cannot stomach the uncertainty and fear that they will reject us. That she Nyx will reject me. We're almost free of the Anhelio compound, but we'll never be truly free of them. We get the girls to safety tonight, but without the proper training, they won't make it out of this alive.

Darkness is coming. True Evil.

And we must be ready for it.

Chapter Five

B onds
Nikki

I am being carried out of the dungeon by the hottest man I have ever seen. I mean fucking drop dead gorgeous. This guy is fucking huge, 6'5", thick blond curls, deep brown eyes, and golden skin covering muscle that goes on for days. I can feel the muscles in his back, and I'm certain his abs are a washboard eight-pack. I'm drooling, and I don't even care.

I can feel the electrical surge that passes between us when he touches me, and I know for certain that I have never felt anything like this in my entire life. I've wanted men before. Probably not with this level of intensity, and definitely not closely following a life or death situation, but I've definitely been a little thirsty for a hot man before.

This isn't that.

This is life changing. This is soul rendering. This is fucking romance novel-level desire, and I simply cannot wrap my mind around why I would suddenly forget that I am in extreme danger. Even though these men appear to have saved us from the monsters who held us hostage for months, we still don't know them from Adam.

Regardless, I am resisting the pull to run my tongue along this man's jaw and lick into his mouth. The desire is engulfing me, and the need feels almost overwhelming, as if I am fighting to keep my head above water suddenly. The longer I stay in his arms, the longer I am engulfed by his unique scent of whiskey and cedar, and the harder it is to remember I don't know him.

We are not lovers, and I sure as hell am not going to beg him to push into me later tonight ... and yet the electricity that is passing between us is profound. I am so enamored with him and the feeling of trust I feel towards a being who not only held a sword to a man's throat, but admitted to being a type of demon, is concerning.

Just as I think about the word *trust* in connection to the man holding me, I feel an acceptance of a truth snap into place, and I shudder as I am pulled under and into a type of dream or vision.

The world becomes dark around me and still. The kind of stillness I have only experienced a handful of times in my life. Like the calmness before a storm or the quiet after it snows. I see myself standing in a type of cave or tall overhang on the side of a desert mountain range. I am dressed in leather armor, and my hair hangs over my shoulders and down my back. I am pacing, and the frustration comes off me in waves.

I look around and see the man who is holding me standing a few feet from me, lounging against the wall of the cave. His back and shoulder are propped against the wall, his knee is bent, and his foot is resting against the wall. He is shirtless, and his skin glows in the early morning light. His muscles ripple in the sunlight, and yet I am unbothered by his near nakedness, almost as if I am comfortable with it.

"Nyx, honestly you have to relax. Your agitation is palpable." He appears bored, and yet his eyes are tired. His exhaustion is almost masked. I stop pacing and stare at him.

"Azrael. Be reasonable. We are losing time. Aliyah and Isaiah are almost fully bonded, and we have only just begun our bonds. We have tried everything to complete the bonds in time and we are failing." My voice is angry and my tone dismissive.

Azrael moves from his relaxed position against the wall to my side in seconds. His scent wraps around me as he pins his body to mine, and I feel my being's acceptance of him immediately. His hands frame my face gently, and his lips cover mine. The surge of feeling that strums through me is reassuring, and I sigh softly as I relax against him.

"Woman, stop," he says as he breaks the kiss and runs his nose along my jaw as he strokes the exposed skin on my arms. "We are not failing.

The bonds are not intended to be done in haste. The surge of power we have experienced as a result of Aliyah and Isaiah moving through their bonding is proof that this is an exceptional thing. It is not to be taken lightly or forced."

"I know this," I reply as he holds me. "But we are running out of time. The gods are no longer with us, and the other Anhelios are disgusting heathens who grow bolder and angrier by the day. Michael will have his war, and we have only completed our first bond." My words confuse me as I hear them.

Azrael sighs. "I realize you are a warrior, Nyx. I know you want to battle your way through every obstacle, but this isn't a war. This is a bonding. It takes time. Trust, acceptance, love ..." His voice trails off as I growl my disapproval at his words.

"And I do accept you as my mate. I trust you above all others. I desire you. What more is there to love than that?" This past version of me pushes away from the man holding me. He shakes his head but allows me to take my space.

"I don't know, woman. Love is a foreign concept to me. We are Anhelios. We do not love or empathize. We do not desire these things. Or we never have before. But I am Aliyah's follower. I agree that the others must be stopped, and I am appalled at the treatment of the humans. I want to be more than we have been. I want to increase our power and with it, our chances of survival if we do go to war with the others. But possibly more than that, I want you. I want your body. Your soul intertwined with mine for all of eternity. Can you say the same?"

I stare at the man in front of me as I feel another piece of the puzzle slide into place. I stride across the room and place my hands on his face as I kiss his mouth, allowing the desire and lust to pulse through my body. "You, my lover, are a genius." I tell him truthfully as I slip my tongue onto his mouth and caress his tongue with my own. He groans beneath me. Azrael lifts me up, and my legs encircle his waist. Our breath syncs, and we stare into each other's eyes as the vision fades.

I stare at the man holding me, and he shudders at the vision ... or possibly memory? I know he saw what I saw and felt what I felt. I know he felt the electricity flowing between us. He says nothing to his friends, and I stare at him in confusion as a sort of promise flows between us.

I quirk an eyebrow, and he puts a finger to his lips in warning. I smile, and after what feels like an eternity I nod my acceptance ... for now. Whatever that was and whatever it means, Azrael doesn't appear to want his friends to know about it.

I damn sure will be demanding answers soon.

· · · ·

We find ourselves at the Demons compound several hours later. It is vastly different from the Anhelios. The Deveon compound is comfortable, lived in, lush with plants, and lots of floor-to-ceiling windows to let the light in, a beautiful outside atrium, pool, and gym. The Anhelio's compound was cold, concrete, and white. With a dungeon. No comparison. It is like night and day. Night being preferable in this scenario.

Kate, Aliyah, and I make ourselves at home on the couches in the living room while the men busy themselves with tasks. Azrael is in the kitchen making tea. Rafa has his back to us as he watches the night slip away in the early morning light, and Isaiah is in a chair across the room. The placement feels intentional.

"Your home is beautiful," I say softly. I don't actually intend to say the words or to compliment the demons, but it is true and helps to break the tension.

"Thank you, little Hunter," Rafa, the funny and charming brother, says with a wink. I watch him with interest. He hasn't actually said much since breaking into our cell and stabbing Gabriel through the heart. Just an obscure comment about being an actual demon on the way out of the Anhelio's torture dungeon.

I wonder if I will feel a connection to him or have visions of knowing him from a past life or whatever. I don't feel anything more than a type of kinship to him.

The Anhelios were repulsive to us. Perhaps because we are Hunters. These Deveons are appealing. Nothing like the electricity I feel with Azrael, but I want to be around them. I feel safe. Which is concerning since they had admitted to being demons just a few hours ago.

"So, you are not evil then?" I ask.

"I mean, sure, of course we are. But it all depends on your view of Good and Evil," Rafa says.

Kate raises a brow. "Do you hurt women and children?"

Rafa scoffs. "I only hurt women who ask me very nicely, and I always try to avoid children at all costs," he says with a shudder.

Kate laughs. "Be serious. I'm truly trying to understand."

I scoff, suddenly angry and resentful towards the men who essentially saved us. "They are fucking demons. They corrupt souls to build armies of warriors for coming battles. What do you need to understand?" I ask my friend sharply. I don't know where the anger has suddenly come from, but I feel it with a sharpness that surprises me. The intensity is off-putting.

Azrael watches me from the kitchen as he pours hot water into large earthenware mugs. His curls fall into his eyes as he pours the water, and his arms flex.

"True. We do. And yet humans enjoy a little corruption and sin. It is not our desire to wipe out your species or to corrupt you to enable you to take yourselves out and do the work for us. That is the Anhelios way," Azrael replies as he hands each of us a cup of tea.

"It's complicated. Anhelios are 'good' in a purity concept. They believe Anhelio blood is better than human blood, and so they wish to dispose of you. It's working too. Through the teaching of purity and elitism, humans believe they are better than one another.

"Deveons are more base and sexual. We enjoy sex, sin, playing, various emotions, and pain," he explains as he settles down next to me. "The concepts of Good and Evil have been forced on humans for millennia. They aren't exactly true concepts though. Humans and celestial beings are complicated. What one being enjoys may not work for another, but if those enjoying it are fine, then who are we to judge?"

Kate nods. "Ok, but slavery, murder, rape? How do you explain these actions if there is no evil?"

Rafa laughs harshly. "Oh, little Hunter. I never said there wasn't evil. True evil in this world absolutely exists. I simply said it isn't what you first perceive it to be. We enjoy all the emotions of human nature; love, desire, sex, diligence, pain, heartbreak. All of this is needed to evolve and become a better or higher version of one's self. If you deny your base instincts because they are wrong, then you can't possibly grow and evolve. All things have aspects of good and evil. It's a matter of degree, is it not?"

"Ok. Assume all that is true. What is your core goal here?" I ask, looking at Azrael.

"Honestly, we are looking for our mates. Before the Angels and Demons were divided and we were sent to hell, there were six of us. The three of us and Aliyah, as well as two more women, Nyx and Keyra. We believed in Aliyah, and she believed that humans should not be used but rather seen as equal. She wanted to live among them and enjoy life.

"This caused a problem with the Anhelios as they wanted to enslave the humans and use them to work the earth. The great divide caused the war between Good and Evil, angering the gods. Now we're looking for Nyx and Keyra and to train the half-human Hunters to help us fight the annihilation of the human race. We hope to find our mates and complete the bonds, making us stronger for the war to come."

"Holy shit, man. That's a lot," I tell the man I am almost certain is my mate. I want to ask if this makes me Nyx and Kate Keyra. If we are the Fallen Warriors they seek, then the Anhelios were right in their assumptions of us. And then they are truly our enemies. We were essentially made to fight them. And to love these men. To befriend one another.

Azrael smiles tightly."Yes, I suppose it is. Regardless, we want to train you. We hope that you might be our lost mates. We won't know until Aliyah and Isaiah complete the bond, and her powers return. Until then, all of you must train. The Anhelios won't be stopped, and now that they know Aliyah has awakened, they will be coming for her after they heal."

I watch Azrael as he delivers this news. "So, you want us to stay here and train. Do we have a choice?" I ask calmly.

"Of course. The decision is yours. You are welcome here. We will train and protect you. If you choose to go, we won't stop you. I can't promise we can help you if the Anhelios find you. We can't sense you without the bonds," Rafa tells them.

Both of us nod. "Cool. Ok well, where do we sleep?" Kate asks, and Rafa laughs.

"I'll show you your rooms," Azrael tells us, effectively ending the night.

There is a kinship here. I am drawn to Aliyah and of course to Azrael. He had said we wouldn't know if we were mates until after Aliyah and Isaiah bonded. I was more than convinced that he and I already knew that we were. Was he keeping that knowledge from his brothers intentionally, and if so, why? Was our status a bad omen for the others?

Chapter Six

Desire
Azrael

As I lead the women to the farthest rooms on the second floor in an attempt to keep Nikki, who I believe is Nyx, away from me for as long as possible, I contemplate how we ended up in this mess to begin with.

We have undoubtedly completed our first bond. I felt the click of the bond falling into place after we pulled them from the Anhelio"s dungeon. She had a vision on the way out of the compound as well. I felt her confusion at our bonding process. Gods, that had been ten thousand years before, and it still felt like yesterday.

"Are you sure our rooms are even on the same property?" Nikki asks me jokingly as we continue along the long corridor away from the living area and Isaiah and Aliyah's suite.

I laugh and allow my arm to brush along hers as we navigate the hallway towards the guest suite at the back of the house. I feel the electric current when our skin touches, and she jumps slightly. I know it was a mistake when Kate side-eyes us and begins to pay more attention to us. I move away from Nikki and smile reassuringly at her.

"I chose the guest rooms to give you privacy and space not only from Rafa and me, but from Isaiah and Aliyah as well. It can be a bit much when a couple is bonding." I tell them truthfully.

Kate looks across at me and nods. "Is it painful to complete the bonds?"

"I'm not sure painful is the right wording. When Alyiah and Isaiah completed their bonds thousands of years ago, we were not in the same dwelling. They had intentionally made their home close to the original garden where the hieroglyphics told the story of the bonds." I tell them truthfully.

"So you don't know?" Kate asks skeptically.

I smile tightly. "I only know what the bonding process was like for my lover and me."

"Wait, you're bonded?" Nikki asks me, as anger and something that feels like hurt color her aura.

"We never completed the bonds. My lover and I had three bonds when the War of the Winged Beasts began. After the gods' punishment, we never saw one another again."

"Are the gods traditional gods?" Kate asks.

I raise a brow, and she waves her hand around.

"Do they orchestrate and pass judgment? Are they simply your gods or do they rule the Anhelios as well? Did they create this world?" she asks with frustration.

"Ah, I see." I tell her and smile softly. "Yes they are traditional gods. More like the Greek gods of mythology and less like your one God. But yes. They rule all of us. Anhelios and Deveons alike, although they do appear to side with the Anhelios as they are the Chosen Ones, and we are the Fallen. They are vengeful and petty at times, and terrifying and all-powerful at others. They did not create this planet. They are celestial beings, but they did create us, the Anhelios."

Kate's eyes widened. "So the gods are aliens?"

I laugh. "Yes, I suppose they are."

"And you are half-alien and half-demigod then?" she says as she swallows hard.

I nod. "*We* are half-alien and half-demigod. You are simply stuck in a human shell of sorts. It is a lot to process. I understand," I tell them softly.

"So Nyx and Keyra are half-alien and half-demigod as well?" Kate asks.

"Yes. They are lost to us at the moment, but perhaps we have found them in you."

"And you and Nyx were bonded and in love?" Kate pushes.

I sigh. "I never intended to fall in love with Nyx. We were Anhelios. Angelic beings. We didn't feel love then, but Alyiah convinced us that enslaving the humans was immoral and wrong. The more we began understanding and empathizing with the humans, the more like them we became."

"So you began to feel love and companionship? Loss and desire? And you wanted more?"

"Yes. The gods had left us an 'out', if you will. A way to bond with one another and become fated mates for eternity. We needed the strength we acquired from the bonding in order to defeat the others. We knew that the Anhelios were growing bolder. Angrier. Our time was running out."

"How did you know you could even form bonds with one another?" Nikki asks skeptically.

"Aliyah called for a coup. She needed an army to fight the Anthelios. There had been whispers of a way to bond and increase our gifts. We discovered the prophecy of the bond shortly before she called us together."

"So Isaiah and Aliyah were lovers?" Kate surmises.

I nod. "Yep. They volunteered to complete the bonding in order to strengthen us. While they were completing their bonds, we acquired telepathy and the ability to travel through dimensions. With the telepathy came the bonding for Nyx and me. We didn't expect the familial bond that came with the deep understanding of one another. The feelings of trust, desire, acceptance, love, respect, and sacrifice were like brands on my skin, and the pull to complete the bonds with Nyx was overwhelming."

Nikki frowns. "So you didn't have a choice? It was just forced on you and your lover?" she asks, appalled.

"Of course we had a choice. The bonds were a gift from the gods. We couldn't complete them if we didn't work like hell to embrace the necessary emotions and process the feelings that came up. We completed three of the bonds thousands of years ago." I watch as Nikki absorbs this information.

Nikki swallows hard, "So you completed three of the six bonds. Is it always the same order? The bonds I mean. Do you have to complete them in order?"

"No. The bonds evolve as the relationship does. All relationships are different."

"What does the completion of the three bonds mean for you and your mate?" Nikki asks.

I watch the woman I am convinced is the reincarnation of my lost lover and smile tightly. "It wasn't enough to help me find her in this world after she was ripped away. It was just enough that she was never out of my head or gone from under my skin. Not enough that I could sense her in her human form though."

Kate gasps. "So the gods punished you by taking your lover?"

I smile at the gentler of the two Hunters and nod. "Yes. To be truthful, it was devastating that the gods had stolen my lover and intended mate from my arms and cast me and my brothers into hell for our roles in attempting to free the humans. It was an unfair punishment when the Anhelios had taken too much and pushed their enslavement of the humans to a form of genocide as they attempted to make a new race of beings loyal only to them."

Kate's face is set in a grimace. "Those fucking Anhelios are even worse than we thought. They essentially damned you."

We became the Fallen, doomed to live an eternity in a hell dimension while our lovers were born again and again in human form with little to no memories of our time together."

Nikki and Kate stare at me in horror. "Fuck. That's so messed up." Nikki breathes out, and Kate nods.

"It is. These are your rooms." I gesture to the doors behind them. "So now you know my story. I hope you can forgive our insistence that you stay and train with us, now that you understand what is at stake."

And they would forgive us. I knew that, just as I knew it wasn't fair or right to ask it. Even though our home was safe and familiar to them, in a sense, it was still a form of capture. I knew that. The woman did not.

We had not intended to trick them, not fully, and yet the wheels had been set in motion. As much as I wanted them to be safe and free to choose their own destiny, I could no longer deny that the need for my mate influenced my decisions. And ultimately their freedom. It was a price I was more than willing to take from them.

Chapter Seven

S ecrets

    Nikki/Nyx

"So, Azrael is hot," Kate says as she inspects the closet of the suite of rooms we were led to. I swallow hard and look around me, ignoring her comments.

The rooms we are standing in are beautiful. The walls are a dove gray with dark charcoal trim and gorgeous drop chandeliers with gold accents. The floors are gray wood with thick cream throw rugs. This room is a shared living space with a beautiful and comfortable looking gray suede couch and a glass and gold coffee table.

I run my hand along the length of the couch and wonder if Azrael would fit on this couch. My incredibly helpful imagination supplies me with an image of him lying down and me straddling his hips. I quickly blink the image away, but not before I imagine his large hands working my hips and my head thrown back in enjoyment. I shake the images away and poke my head into the room Kate has disappeared into.

This room is similar to the living area, but the color scheme is darker. Charcoal bedspread, pillows and curtains, gold light fixtures and pulls on the black lacquered dressers and nightstands. Kate is standing at the floor-to-ceiling window with the curtain pulled back, watching the sunrise color the desert.

"Do you think they have wings like the Anhelios?" she asks softly without looking at me.

I nod anyway. "Yes."

She swallows hard. "And Alyiah?"

I shake my head. "No. She's human. I think she probably will if she and Isaiah complete the bonding."

"What about you and me?" Kate turns away from the window and gives me a shaky smile.

"I don't know. If we're their mates, and that's a huge *if*, then yeah, we probably will. I hadn't even thought of that. I suppose this is all unfolding really fast." I reach for my friend and squeeze her shoulders in a hug.

"You like him, huh?" she asks softly, and I hug her tighter.

"I do." I reply without thinking it through.

"Gods, you should see the way he looks at you."

I laugh and release her from the hug. "And how exactly does he look at me?"

"Like he's dying of thirst and you're a pool of clear blue water." She smirks.

"Shut the fuck up. He does not."

"He most certainly fucking does. And you look at him like you've never seen a damn man before. I swear I can see you thinking about climbing him like a fucking tree and sitting on his face."

I laugh and push my friend away. "Gods, woman you have an active imagination. Even if I do want him, it's a bad idea. Aliyah and Isaiah have to complete their bonds before we know for sure that we are even fated mates. Plus there's a fucking apocalypse brewing, and we're going to need all the training we can get if we're going to help fight the Anhelios. And I'd really like to fucking destroy them for the months of psychological torture we endured in that damn dungeon."

Kate smiles tightly at me. "Yes. I hope we do get superhero demon powers. I'd love to have the strength to hurt them. Very slowly."

I stare at my friend. "Youre kinda fucking scary you know that?"

She laughs. "I hope so. I'm really fucking tired of being a punching bag." She heads for the door to the right of the bedrooms, correctly assuming it's the washroom. "I'm gonna take a quick shower. Something tells me the water pressure here is going to be worth the wait."

I laugh at my friend's quick change of topic and groan inwardly at the thought of a hot shower. "Take your time. I'm going to guess that they spared no expense on the hot water heater."

Kate laughs. "Good point," she calls through the open door as she turns on the water and begins to undress. "So we're staying here, Nik ... even if they are literal demons?" she asks, poking her head out of the open door.

"I think it's the safest place for us. At least for now. If they trigger even the slightest run factor, we go. And the Anhelios were literal angels, and they were terrifying. I think Azrael is right, it's time to change our thought process on Good versus Evil."

Kate smiles. "All teasing aside, I like Azrael for you. He is the calm to your crazy, hot as fuck, and patient. Isaiah is a little scary. I hope Aliyah knows what she is doing there."

I watch my friend curiously as she moves away from the door to test the water temperature. She is wrapped in a soft, plush, black towel. "And Rafa?" I ask.

Kate doesn't look away from the flow of water. She swallows hard. "I hope we aren't fated mates. He is really sexy, and I don't know, almost beautiful and so funny, but he is also cold and I think, maybe mean?" She turns her head to meet my eyes. "I get the undeniable impression that he really doesn't like me. He absolutely doesn't look at me like I'm a cold refreshing pool of water, so maybe you and Aliyah are Fallen, but I don't think I am. And that's ok. I am good with being a Hunter. I'm good with helping you find the other Deveon warriors and helping to stop Michael and those assholes from destroying humanity. Now go away. I am dying for this shower." I leave her to her shower and close the door behind me. I am worried for my friend but also aware that she may be right. We might just be Hunters, and any feelings I have for Azrael will be stomped

out when he finds his true mate.

"You are my true mate." The voice is soft but also tinged with annoyance. The fact that it is Azrael is obvious to me, and yet I still jump slightly. He moves out of the shadows and guides me toward the back bedroom. My skin tingles with his nearness.

He pins me against the wall and runs his nose along the length of my throat. I shiver at the feel of him, my body subconsciously pressing against his. He rests his hands on my hips, his long fingers grazing against my ass as I feel the hardness of his body against mine. My breasts feel heavy, and my nipples pebble under my shirt. Our mouths are just inches apart, and I desperately want to close the distance and lick his lips, his tongue, his hot, wet mouth.

Azrael groans and grinds against me.

My brain short circuits for a moment. "Please ..." I whisper as I sink my fingers into his thick curls and raise my mouth to his.

He groans. "Please what? Kiss you? Own you?" His hand slips between my thighs to cup my wet core. "Push inside your tight wet cunt and bond with you for eternity?" he asks cruelly as I grind my hips against his hand and find his mouth

"Yes," I reply as the kiss deepens. Azrael slips his hand to my throat and pushes me further against the wall, his mouth out of reach again as he strokes the softness of my throat.

"I want to, Nikki. I really do, but we have to be careful. You need to understand the implications of all this before we make any life-changing decisions. We already completed the first bond when we saved you and you trusted me. I can hear your thoughts." He winks.

I can feel my skin heat. "Wait, what?"

Azrael smirks. "The naughtier the thoughts, or the more intense, the more you project. Aliyah projects to all of us. Most likely because she is our leader, but I can hear and see what you are projecting too." Azrael squeezes my throat and then releases me.

"So only you know what I'm projecting?"

"I could see your memories of us and your thoughts of us just a few moments ago on the couch. I could also feel your anguish and pain when you thought about the Anhelios."

"Will I be able to hear you, if you project?" I ask curiously

"Yes. I can block my thoughts if I don't want you to hear or feel them, and you can learn to do that too. Nyx and I completed three bonds. She could hear me immediately, but I imagine being in a human form limits your ability."

"What if I'm not her?" I ask, my words thick.

"If you aren't Nyx? How would you have her memories if you weren't her?" Azrael looks thoughtful. "The gods are deceptive and sneaky. But I've never felt anything like the connection I have with you except with Nyx when we decided to fall in love ..."

"What, when you *decided* to fall in love? How do you decide to fall in love?" I ask, thoroughly confused.

"We were celestial beings, Nikki. We didn't have emotions the way you and even I do now. This was ten thousand years ago. We chose to fall in love. But make no mistake, we were desperately in love. You were mine and I was yours. When the gods stole you from me, I absolutely lost my shit. No control, just rage. I will not lose you again."

The intensity with which he declares it sends a shiver down my spine, and Azrael drops a kiss on my shoulder and presses his body tighter to mine.

"I know the others would want us to wait for Isaiah and Aliyah. If we complete three bonds, there is no going back. If we complete four and you decide you don't want me or Aliyah and Isaiah never finish their bonds, I will lose my ability to reason. It would render me useless in the fight to save humanity." His voice trails off as his mouth captures mine again.

I groan. "This is torture."

His hands skim over my body. His tongue trails over mine and then sucks gently. I tighten my arms around his neck and encircle my legs around his hips when his big hands grip my ass and lift me. I envision my hands unzipping his jeans and sliding inside to grip his long, thick shaft.

Azrael shudders. "And then?" he asks, his voice thick.

I grind my core against him and imagine his hands sliding under my shirt to pinch and twist my nipples. His teeth graze my earlobe as I envision sliding down his body and looking up at him with big, expectant eyes.

Azrael groans again as I think of him taking himself into his large hand and giving his cock a few hard tugs before gently tapping my thick lips with the head of his cock, demanding entrance. I open my mouth and lick the salty tip as he pushes the head into my open mouth. "Wider."

I nod as I imagine opening my mouth as wide as I can to accommodate his large, thick cock. I think of licking and sucking as he pushes more of himself into my throat, and I choke a bit on it.

Azrael unbuttons my jeans and slides his hand into my pants, his thick fingers finding my clit and rubbing gentle circles as he groans, "Finish me, woman."

He growls into my ear as he slips a thick digit inside me. I groan and imagine him sliding in and out of my mouth as I increase the suction, desperate to feel him cum down my throat. Azrael shudders as he holds back his orgasm and increases the thrust of his fingers inside me. We hear the shower turn off, and Kate moving around in the washroom.

I groan, and Azrael smiles a wolfish grin as he lifts my shirt and bites my nipple just hard enough to make me cry out. I'm still gripping him tightly when he kisses my neck and removes his hand gently, setting me on my feet.

"I'll go before she catches me. But Nikki, I'm gonna need you to climb on that bed and imagine us finishing that, in detail. No distractions. I want you to come. I fucking need you to. Do you understand?"

I nod, my body in complete agreement with his demands. "Do you want to come inside me, or ...?" I ask shamelessly.

Azrael stares at me, his eyes darkening, and then licks his lips. "Give me ten minutes to get back to my room, and honestly baby, it's your show. I have no doubt you will blow my mind." He kisses me and then strides to the window, opens the clasp, and drops out of view.

Chapter Eight

Restraint
Azrael

"No. I need you to strike out, Nikki. Put your weight into it and drive the punch home," I demand as I spar with the human woman who I am convinced embodies my Deveon mate.

She steps forward and strikes my side with her full body weight. I smile and rub the spot where she struck me.

"Good. More," I tell her as she dances back and strikes out again connecting with my lower abs. This time, the impact has more of a sting, and I nod and dance around her. She smiles softly and sweeps out a leg to knock me off my feet and onto my back. I hit the mats with a thud.

I laugh and smile up at her. She nods down at me beneath her, and I groan at the darkness in her eyes.

"Keep pushing. You're doing better, but I need you to concentrate and keep your focus. Hunters need to be faster and stronger than both Angels and Demons. Your life depends on it."

Nikki watches me and then steps over me and lowers down so that she is squatting over me, and I breathe in the scent of her skin. Her long hair brushes my shoulder, and I stifle another groan as she moves her body over mine and drops to her knees above me. She is so close now that I can feel the heat of her body just inches from mine.

"I can keep my focus, Az. Not a problem. I can push back too, if you want that. But this, right here, is fucking killing me. You need to push back and give me what we both want. I promise my concentration will be on point," she tells me with a look that stops my breath in my lungs.

Before I can stop myself, my hands are on her hips, and I am pushing my hardness up and into the cradle of her thighs. I rub against the heat of her core as she drops her chest to mine. I can feel the roundness of her breasts and her tight nipples as she works against me. I flip her without thought and push my body hard against her as I trap her beneath me. My mouth is just inches from hers, and I gently lick the corner of her mouth as she gasps.

"Trust me, love. I want to. I really do. This is fucking killing me too, babe. Watching you touch that sweet pussy over our bond might be the death of me. But we have to wait. We have to give Alyiah the chance to choose."

Her heartbeat quickens, and she rubs her body against mine. She arches her back to make full contact, and I growl as she wraps her legs around my hips and bites her lip.

"I want you, Azrael. I've never needed someone like this, and honestly it's scaring me. Can't we fuck without bonding? I need this," She whispers softly.

I watch her eyes. "Damn, baby. I wish that was possible, but when I get inside that pussy I'm not holding back, and the way I feel when I'm near you, Nikki—I doubt the Gods themselves could stop another bond from happening." I kiss the corner of her mouth and pinch her nipple hard. She shudders and closes her eyes tightly.

"Damn it, Azrael. Why can't this just be a good time?" she asks with resentment and a healthy dose of anger in her voice. I laugh as I roll off her and stand up, pulling her with me.

"Some things are bigger than that, babe," I tell her, and her eyes slip down to my sweats as I laugh. "Fucking dirty girl."

"Aliyah better fucking choose Isaiah before I lose my shit," she mumbles as she steps back from me and then springs over the boxing ring ropes to land a perfect backflip. I laugh out loud and nod at her expertise.

"Perhaps frustration is good for you, babe. It seems to sharpen your focus, and we're going to need that to fight the Anhelios."

She flips me off and heads out of the gym. I smile at her antics and grab my towel and water bottle. I turn just as Rafa enters the gym. He nods to me and shoots his eyes to the door as if questioning Nikki. I nod at my chosen brother.

"What's the story there?" he asks lightly, and I groan. I haven't mentioned the bond with Nikki to either of my brothers, and the half lies are driving me crazy.

"What if Nikki is Nyx and Kate really is Keyra?"

"It's possible. Keyra and I never bonded before the War of the Winged Beasts so I can't sense her. If Alyiah is our queen, then the bonds should begin for us once she and Isaiah get their heads out of their asses. Why? You feeling Nikki?"

I shake my head at my friend and smile. "She's amazing. I'm enthralled with her fighting skills and her tenacity."

He nods and looks toward the empty doorway. "It's a forever thing though, man. If she's your woman, then that's it. She's the only one for all of eternity. You good with that?" I sense his reluctance for his own bonds.

I slap him on the back and grip his shoulder. "I'm honestly more concerned with the possibility that Nikki isn't my fated mate, and I can't have her for all of eternity."

Rafa throws his head back and laughs. "Damn. You do have it bad." I laugh. "Ok. Full transparency. Nikki and I bonded the first night we rescued them."

Rafa stares at me for ten whole seconds before he bursts out laughing again. "Seriously? Good gods, you move fast. That was weeks ago though. Nothing since?"

I swallow hard. "No. We bonded over the savior aspect and nothing physical. I believe it was the trust bond.The bond created a telepathy between us. I can hear and feel her thoughts. She can't open her side of the bond yet though."It feels good to get this off my chest. I watch my brother as he processes this information.

"Ok. So you can hear and feel her thoughts. That's good, right? We can sense them now and know when they are hurt or in danger."

I smile. "Yes. I also know when she needs something else ..."

"Gods, man, you are so fucked. Ok, so help a girl out. Maybe she just wants a good time ..." His voice trails off as he notices the anger etched across my features. "You aren't attracted to her?" he asks, surprised.

I sigh. "Nope. That's really not the problem."

"Ok, so what is the problem?"

"You really don't know how the bond works at all?" I ask my friend with surprise.

"Nope. Sorry man, I just don't care. I never wanted to be with one woman for eternity. Sounds terrible, honestly."

"Fair enough. Although if Kate is Keyra, you really will need to bond with her for us to achieve our full powers ... just saying."

Rafa shakes his head "We'll see. Isaiah isn't faring all that well with Aliyah, so I'm thinking it may not be a problem for me."

"True, which is a huge problem for humanity. You know if they don't complete the bonds, then we don't get Aliyah back, and quite honestly, we're not exactly saving humanity without her. Also Nyx and I are at a standstill until we get our girl back." I tell him, entirely too unhappy with that reality.

Rafa laughs. "Ok, Romeo, relax. Why don't you and Nikki have a little fun until Aliyah and Isaiah figure their shit out?"

I groan. "A little fun is killing me. Please don't forget that we can only have three bonds before there is no going back. I will literally go insane from the pain, and if Nikki is Nyx, then she will suffer as well. I'm not doing that. And if I haven't been clear, this is hell for me."

Rafa laughs. "Sounds like all of that is a problem for later. And if I remember correctly, you enjoyed hell. It wasn't all bad there. Everyone makes it out to be some sort of torture chamber but we had some good times before our eventual jailbreak. Damn, man, live a little."

Rafa moves towards the training equipment at the back of the gym, and I make my way to the showers.

"Oh and Alyiah and Isaiah have a date tonight, so I think it's safe to say those two are on the right track. Have fun with your girl man, what's the worst that can happen?" Rafa yells to my retreating back as I head out.

I growl at his nonchalance and consider my options.

Since Nikki and I bonded and discovered the telepathy bond, we have been playing sex games for weeks now. This shit is literally killing me. I know we have to hit the brakes or bite the bullet and complete the next bond.

After my talk with Rafa, I'm leaning towards completing the next bond. It can't be any worse than what we are experiencing now, and Rafa isn't wrong. The closer I get to my fated mate, the better chance we have of protecting all the girls.

It's been three weeks, and she is literally driving me crazy. I need to feel the softness of her skin, to have her scent around me. I can't stand the mental orgasms anymore. I want her under me, over me. All of it. I want to actually taste her. I know it's wrong, but if Aliyah and Isaiah are over their standstill, then maybe Nikki and I can afford to get physical without the risk of losing her when they inevitably fall apart. At least, that's what I try telling myself as I head to the showers. Unfortunately for me, Alyiah is about to discover a truth that will all but destroy our plans.

Chapter Nine

The Seduction
Nikki

"Hold still, woman!" I tell Alyiah with more humor than annoyance as she blinks rapidly and shakes my hands from her face.

"Good gods, Nik, I asked you for help, not to blind me!" Aliyah exclaims as I roll my eyes.

"Don't be so dramatic. Trust me, when you see the magic I just worked on your face, you're going to be worshiping the ground I walk on." I laugh as I lightly grip her jaw and turn her face up to finish her eyeliner.

Aliyah snorts, and Kate laughs from the plush chair in the corner. She is sorting through the dresses we pulled for Aliyah's first real date with Isaiah tonight. I am currently finishing her makeup. We went with a glam style, and she looks like a model from the 1920's with her lush curls and dark eyes. Her red lips curl into a smile as she watches me.

"You've been awfully quiet, Nik. Are you thinking about Az?" she asks with a wicked smile.

I step back and swallow my nerves at her question. I am surprised at her candor, as I thought we had done a good job of hiding our growing bond over the past month.

"Why would I be thinking about Azrael?" I ask her as Kate snorts from her chair. I brandish the curling iron as I wrap sections of her hair around the barrel and feign innocence.

"Come on girl, we all know you want to climb that man like a tree and ride his face like a banshee." She tries to peek around me in the mirror.

I step in her way and smile harshly. "Nope, no peeking until the look is finished ... Like a banshee huh?" The skepticism in my voice is clear.

Aliyah winks. "You know, how banshees scream in exhilaration ... anyway, I don't hear you denying the comment about climbing the man and riding his face."

I choke on air and wrap another section of her hair around the curler. "Clearly. Have you seen the man? Who wouldn't want to ride that face?" Both women laugh.

"I have to say, while Azrael is gorgeous, he does seem to only have eyes for you, girl. And personally, I wouldn't mind having a go at Rafa. I can't shake the intensity there, even if he does have a one and done vibe about him." Kate says softly from her chair.

I glance over at my friend and toss her a wicked smile. "Damn girl. I didn't know you had it in you." I'm impressed with her boldness.

Kate shrugs. "I actually don't, but I wouldn't mind having it in me," Kate mumbles, and Aliyah and I burst out laughing.

Kate untangles herself from her place on the chair and steps up to Aliyah with a gorgeous red satin dress. "Ok, step into this one. Let's see if it has that 'Come and get me, big boy' vibe that we all know you're secretly going for," Kate tells Aliyah with a wink.

Aliyah laughs. "Or not so secretly. I think we all know if this date goes well, I'll be shamelessly begging for it later tonight."

We all laugh, and I bite back the desire to tell them I was literally begging Azrael for it earlier today. I step out of the way and survey my friend. She looks breathtaking, and I truly hope things go well for her and Isaiah tonight.

"I'm happy for you, Aliyah. You deserve to be pampered, and despite his rough edges, I do think Isaiah adores you."

Aliyah turns to me with tears in her eyes and wraps me in a tight hug. "Thank you, Nik. For your warm wishes but also for working your magic. I look so beautiful."

I bark out a surprised laugh. "Girl, have you seen you? You are always breathtaking," I tell her as I squeeze her back.

Aliyah smiles and turns away from her reflection. "I could honestly say the same about both of you."

"Well, obviously." I roll my eyes. Aliyah laughs again and slips into the heels Kate hands her.

"Ok, it's now or never," Aliyah says with a nervous smile, and Kate and I watch her as she heads out the door to find Isaiah. "Try to behave while I'm gone ladies."

"No promises!" I call out a little too truthfully at her back. We can hear her laughter as she heads down the steps.

Kate squeezes my hand. "I'm going to suggest to Rafa that we head out for more supplies tonight. Give you and Azrael some alone time. Take it, Nik. Even if we're not the Deveon Warriors they are looking for, I am 100 percent sure that man will give you a night you won't easily forget."

I laugh and squeeze her hand back. "I have to say you are way more perceptive than I thought you were ... or I'm way less sneaky than I thought."

"No, you are incredibly sneaky. I'm assuming you've been up to something with that man for weeks because the way he looks at you ... damn. It's like he's a tortured soul roaming around in a delicious body. Whatever you are doing to him, keep it up, girl." She laughs as she heads out of the room, presumably to find Rafa.

• • • •

I am not trying to seduce Azrael. Well, not entirely.

I heard Rafa and Kate head out about ten minutes ago, and I might have found a skimpy bathing suit that is exactly the perfect color of teal to bring out the gold tones of my skin. It is also just small enough to show most of my skin without giving away the good parts.

I grab a tiny, white wrap-around coverup that barely covers my ass and a fluffy black towel and then head down to the pool. I tell myself I'm just going to get in a few laps and try to relax while everyone else is out of the house. But the way the butterflies are swirling around in my stomach, I'm fairly certain I'm not fooling anyone, least of all, myself.

I hope I'm not broadcasting too much desire as I find my way through the halls and out to the atrium. It's so beautiful here. The sun is just setting and the golds, pinks, and oranges are saturating the sky as I step out into the covered space.

I love the desert and am truly grateful that the universe brought me here at this time in my life. I breathe in deeply and slowly unwrap my coverup. Letting it drop on the steps behind me, I can sense Azrael nearby and am shamelessly giving him a bit of a show. I raise my arms over my head and stretch, allowing my full breasts to stretch the fabric of the top a bit.

I can feel his eyes on me, and I try to hide my smile as I move into the water. I love the feel of the cold pool water against my heated skin. and I slip into the deeper water, allowing the cold water to cover my chest and then springing up a bit onto my toes so that the water drips off my chest and my hard nipples are visible through the fabric.

I hear the splash behind me before I see him, and I know Azrael is coming for me. I laugh softly, thinking he didn't wait long, when I feel strong arms behind me and a hard chest against my back.

"I can feel how much you want me, darling. It isn't nice to tease." The words are whispers against my ear, and I shiver. Azrael groans and slides his hands up from my waist and over both breasts. His fingers tease my erect nipples, and I groan softly when he presses his hard cock against my ass.

"I want a taste, baby. Let me taste you, Nikki," he growls against my ear, and I can feel my thighs grow slick with my desire.

"Please," I moan as I open my legs wider, and he slips his hand over my mound, his fingers teasing along the edges of my bikini bottoms. Azrael quickly slips the bottoms off and possessively holds my pussy in his cupped hand as he sucks at my neck and ear. His erection presses against my ass.

He gently lifts me up onto my toes so that his cock is slanted between my thick thighs. I squeeze my legs together gently, and he bites my ear. I can feel him throbbing between my legs, and I circle my hips gently to feel more of him against me.

Azrael laughs harshly and grips my hips tightly in his hands. "I said I want to taste you, babe. No distractions." His voice is gravelly with desire. I nod slightly and allow him to guide me to the waterfall in the pool. He ducks me beneath the water, and I find myself in a secluded pool behind the waterfall with a gently sloping edge.

I move towards the platform with Azrael still pressed behind me. He raises my arms and drapes them over his neck as he continues suckling the sensitive skin along my neck. His hands stroke my breasts and hips until I can't take it anymore, and I gyrate against his hard, slick member trapped between my thighs. He feels so good, and I only regret it when I feel the hard pinch of his fingers on my nipples.

"It's my show now, Nik. I say when you move, baby. I say when you get off. Do you understand?" I bite my lip hard and nod. His hands slide lower, gently slipping over my mound and stroking my clit. I moan and hear the sound echo off the water and stone around me.

I stand completely still as Azrael guides his hard cock over my wet pussy as his large, calloused finger presses into my clit, rubbing in hard strokes as he drives me up. I grip his thick blond hair in my clenched hands and imagine his lips closing over my nipple.

I hear his chuckle as he licks the skin along my neck and gently turns me to face him, "So fucking greedy, baby," he murmurs as he arranges his cock between my legs again, gently pushing against my folds as he lowers his mouth to bite my nipple through the bikini top. He nudges the fabric away and closes his lips over my nipple as I untie the top and let it float away.

I move my hips back and catch the tip of his cock at my center just before I thrust forward and take him inside. He pinches the delicate skin of my inner thigh, and I freeze, the pain sharp against my desire.

"I said, I will decide when, Nikki. I am in charge now." He grips my hips and lowers me to the stone platform. I groan and wiggle beneath him, but he holds me in place. "Do I need to teach you a lesson, babe, or can you behave?"

"Fuck, that's hot," I tell him, and he presses his hand to my throat, holding me in place while he grips his cock in his other hand.

"Open," he tells me, and I open my mouth greedily. Azrael lifts me by my throat until I am on my knees, and then he presses the tip of his huge cock into my mouth and against my tongue.

I open wider, and he pushes the full length inside, slowly forcing himself to the back of my throat. He tightens his hand on my throat as he works himself deeper down my throat. My eyes water, and my pussy throbs.

"Touch yourself, baby," he tells me as I suck at his cock and work my clit desperately. I want him so damn badly.

"God's, woman, don't stop sucking," he demands as he pushes deeper, and I groan with lust. Azrael moves gently in and out of my mouth, faster as I suck harder at his cock, and he pushes two fingers inside my pussy.

"Nikki, fuck. That's so good," he growls as he comes down my throat, and I shudder with longing as I swallow him down.

Moments later, as my mouth is still suckling him, Azrael pulls himself from my throat and pushes me back so I am lying on the stone again. He strokes my throat lovingly as he forces his head between my thighs and then gently licks my clit.

I arch off the stone, greedy and desperate, so full of lust and desire I can feel my mind and body unraveling. He holds me down by my throat and licks deeper. I can feel his laughter against my core, and I sink my fingers into his thick hair and hold on as I come completely undone.

The pool water slaps against the slab of stone I am reclined on, and the waterfall crashes just a few feet away as I slowly come back to myself and to Azrael who has joined me on the extended platform, his arm under my head as my body curls into him. I smile lazily at the man next to me as my heart thumps loudly, and I feel myself falling.

The sensation of falling is strong, and I hear a slight buzzing in my ears as my vision fades, and then the image before me comes into focus. It is Azrael and me, and yet not this version of us. An older version, something from long ago.

Azrael looks different. His thick blond hair is long and wavy past his bronze shoulders, and huge golden wings extend from his shoulder blades. He is pacing back and forth before me. Gone is the calm and stoic man I know now. This version of him is passionate and angry. I watch in silence as Azrael fumes.

"Aliyah is right. The others are dispassionate and cruel. We cannot allow them to rape and violate the humans in some form of twisted genocide." I watch him and frown slightly. He stops pacing and comes to me. I reach up to touch his face, so beautiful and angelic. "You disagree, my Nyx? We should stand aside and allow this to continue to happen?"

I shake my head and smile sadly at my lover. "No. I do not disagree. Aliyah is right. You are right. We must fight them and stop this disgusting display of power and abuse," I tell him sadly as his hands come up to frame my face.

"Then why so much sadness in your aura, my love?" he asks as he touches his fingertips to my lips.

"It will be a long and difficult battle, Azrael," I tell him honestly. "This experiment of the gods has been horrific and terrifying. I miss the days when it all seemed to make sense. When we had a purpose."

Azrael watches me, his eyes flickering back and forth across my face. "What purpose did we have, Nyx? To guard the humans? To breed them and enslave them? To keep them uneducated and simple? How was that purpose something more than the purpose we have now ... to protect them and empower them?" Azrael's thumbs gently stroke my face gently as he talks.

I sigh and begin to pace. "I'm not saying this isn't a noble cause. It is, and I am committed. But I feel the lack of power, Az. Can't you feel it? It's as if the gods themselves have abandoned us. We need to find a way to increase our power, or we will never defeat the other Anhelios. We will lose without an advantage. Aliyah is strong and wise. She is a true leader, and I would die for her cause, but we need more than her ability to gather followers. We must find an advantage."

Azrael catches my hand and pulls me to him. I am much smaller than him, and the power of his embrace lands me against his chest. He holds me for a moment, and then he kisses me.

The kiss is deep and passionate. His tongue presses against my sealed lips, requesting entrance. I relent and open my lips only to have his tongue sweep inside and claim me. My knees weaken, and my heart trips at the feel of him.

What we have is so much more than just sex. More than the coming together of bodies that we were when we first began to indulge in the pleasures of the flesh. I long for him. For the essence of him. Something in this man makes me feel whole. Honored. Loved.

I match his kiss with my own, our teeth and lips clashing as we come together. It's a battle of sorts. Azrael nips at my lips and strokes my back, my hair, my wings, and my throat. I calm in his arms. He lifts his face from my shoulder.

"I think I found something, Nyx," he says softly, and I hold my breath. He sighs. "There is a prophecy. It is written on the walls of a cave near the first garden." His voice fades away, and I pull back slightly to look at him.

"What type of prophecy?"

Azrael swallows hard. "It speaks of a bonding between lovers. There are six bonds, and once they have been achieved, the lovers become one. Fated mates who will be bonded for eternity. If these Anhelios accomplish a true and complete bonding, then they will unlock unimaginable power and gifts. The prophecy speaks of six Anhelios who are destined to bond and save humanity."

We stare at each other.

I swallow hard and smile at my lover. "And you want to do this? You want to become two of these bonded Anhelios in order to save humanity?"

Azrael nods. "This could be our true calling. It could potentially undo all the bad that we have done in helping to enslave the humans in the beginning."

I watch him, my hands still planted on his chest. I take a deep breath and let it out slowly. "You want to be bound to me for all of eternity?" I am both repulsed and impressed at the same time.

"I can think of no other soul I would prefer to be bound to for all eternity. I can think of no other body I would want to be engulfed in for the rest of my long life. I can think of no other mate who I would want to share this existence with." Azrael kisses my lips and drops to his knees before me. "Please, Nyx, my lover, my friend, my mate, please do me the honor of allowing me to love and protect you for all eternity."

I laugh at this ridiculously large man kneeling before me, begging for my love. My eyes fill with tears. "I do not need protection, you fool. I am one of the most powerful warriors in all of existence," I scoff. "But I do love you, Azrael. Somehow during this sexual awakening of ours, I lost my mind and gave you the only thing I own worth protecting, my heart."

He stands and lifts me in the air. "I love you. I will always love you, Nyx. You are mine, and I am yours for all eternity."

The tears slip down my face as I smile at this man, this being that I love more than any other.

"You are mine, and I am yours." I repeat as the vision fades to black.

I snap back to the present with a start and stare in confusion at the man next to me. He lovingly strokes my hair, my face, and my throat.

"This was how we once were?" I ask him as I stare at this being who was once my sole purpose for existing. Someone I loved more deeply than I would have thought possible.

He smiles down at me. His eyes are unbearably sad. "Yes. We were once so deeply in love we would have moved heaven and earth for the chance to be together. Hell, we did. We just didn't succeed."

I return his smile. "Was that a vision?" I ask him, humbled by the experience.

"Yes. It was a vision. It was also the completion of our second bond." I cover my mouth in shock, and he smiles at me. Azrael removes my hands and gently kisses the corners of my mouth. "Was it too much?" he asks, trying to read my response.

I nod and then shake my head. "No. I mean, it was a lot. Don't get it twisted, but I can handle it."

"And this?" Azrael gestures to the space between us.

I smile and catch his hand as I pull him closer to me. "This, I can definitely handle it. This is nothing short of amazing. This ..." I tell him as I press my mouth to his, "... completely blew my mind, and I want to do this for as long as humanly possible."

Azrael laughs. "Ok. Let's go with that." He returns my kiss and then swoops me up into his arms and carries me back through the waterfall. He sets me down on the lounge chair next to the water and wraps me in a huge, soft, black towel while he collects my very small bikini as it floats in the pool.

Exiting the water in nothing but bronze skin and well defined muscles, I try not to drool as he shakes the water from his hair and wraps a towel around his waist. "Are you hungry?" he asks and smiles as I nod enthusiastically. "Ok babe, why don't you get dressed, and I'll make us something."

For the rest of the evening, I try incredibly hard not to think of what will happen if this somehow all falls apart. I'm not generally a negative person. I usually hope for the best and plan for the worst.

And yet something deep inside whispers to me to be careful with my heart. I trust Azrael. I definitely desire him, but my soul whispers caution. I'm just not sure if I plan on listening.

Chapter Ten

The Loss

Azrael

I wake up holding the only woman I have ever loved. I am certain now that Nikki is the human embodiment of my Anhelio-turned-Deveon lover, Nyx. Our second bond and Nikki's vision following the bond are proof that she is my mate.

Nikki is different from my Nyx in so many ways. They look different, of course, and they have had different life experiences. Nikki is human, and that makes her weaker and less aware of our immortal ways. And yet she has the same captivating force about her. She is inspiring and powerful in her own way. I stretch and smile down at the gorgeous woman who is beginning to trust—and maybe someday love—me again.

Her eyes flutter open, and she yawns. "No one ever said anything about love, big boi. Give a girl a minute to catch up." She has enough snark to stop a train.

I laugh. "No one actually said anything at all, darling," I tell her pointedly as I drop a kiss on her head.

"Wait, what?" Nikki exclaims as she sits up and scoots back on the bed so that her back is resting against the headboard. "You didn't say anything out loud?" she asks excitedly.

I smile. "No. I'm going to have to guard my thoughts. Apparently, you can share the telepathy bond with me after our second bond." I wink.

Nikki punches my shoulder and scrambles onto my lap. "Think something," she demands as she straddles my lap and stares into my eyes expectantly.

I bite back a smile, knowing full well the Deveon Warrior in my lap would never approve of how adorable I find her scrunched up face and inquisitive eyes.

Instead, I send her the image I have of her sliding out of her coverup at the edge of the pool last night, her apple-shaped ass peeking out from her bikini bottoms and the muscles of her back contracting as she slips the wraparound dress down her arms. Her bronze skin glows in the late afternoon light, and I think about gently biting the smooth skin just below her ass.

"Oh. This is what it was like for you when I sent you thoughts?" She is a bit breathless as she settles her ass against my hardness and closes the distance between our mouths. "I think I like this game even better now," she says softly as her pink tongue flicks out to lick my lips.

I groan and place my hands on her hips as she gently rocks her body back and forth. Suddenly the house rocks, and we hear crashing from Isaiah and Aliyah's room. I hold Nikki close, instinctively covering her body with mine as I listen for intruders. Instead, I can clearly hear Aliyah in my mind as she projects her anger and disappointment at Isaiah.

"Oh, there's no need to explain now, Isaiah. I finally understand. You knew I would fucking die when your queen comes back, and you didn't tell me."

Aliyah's voice is strong and incredibly angry.

I can feel my mate stiffen in my arms as I swallow hard and meet Nikki's eyes. "What the actual fuck, Azrael?" she asks softly.

I groan inwardly as I remove myself from her. Nikki springs up and finds her clothes. "Is Aliyah saying that the Demon Queen you all worship is going to take Aliyah's body if she is awakened? Is your mate going to consume my essence if we complete the bonds?" Her voice is strangely strangled as she steps into her pants.

I cringe. "We don't actually know what will happen when our Deveon mates are reborn," I tell her honestly.

She stares at me and then numbly pulls her shirt over her head and shakes out her hair. "Ok. Wow. I'm going to say that was a gross and negligent gloss over of our eventual non-existence. But hey, a demons gotta do what a demons gotta do right?" she asks, her voice oddly cold.

I can feel the hurt radiating from her body, and for the first time, I regret her new-found ability to hear our projections. It's stupid. She would have found out eventually. And the truth is, she does deserve to know that we simply don't know what will happen to the women they are now when their true essence is restored.

"Honestly, Nik, my best guess is that your essence will join with your original soul when you are fully restored. You'll be you. Just ... more."

She blinks at me. "Your best guess? Well, shit. Nothing to worry about here, just a couple of women overreacting to their potential demise." Nikki pushes past me and heads for the door. "Ok, Az. I think it's safe to say we're done here. Thank you for the orgasms. Good times. Let's keep this drastic mistake to ourselves, yeah?" She has enough anger to drive her point home.

I reach for her, the very real possibility that I will lose her again crashing into me. "Babe, no. We're not through here. You are my other half. You're it for me." My voice is tight with fear and regret.

Nikki looks at me with sadness and an acceptance that tears at my heart. "Come on, Azrael. Be real for a moment. Our entire relationship hangs on the very slim possibility that Aliyah and Isaiah can get through their shit and complete the bonds. There is no us without them, and I gotta tell you *babe*, it doesn't look good for us even without the lies and half truths. Forget the potential death sentence for a moment. I can't be with someone when it's not even real between us without someone else's reality affecting ours. This is crazy." She pulls away from me and reaches for the door. "I'm not second to anyone. Not even the Queen of the Damned," she tells me tightly, and I nod as I let her go.

Nyx would never have allowed what we were to be determined or defined by another's definition of love or relationship. It absolutely tracks that this would be a non-starter for her human counterpart as well.

Frustrated, I run my hands through my hair and tug at the roots as I take a deep breath. I sit on the edge of the bed and breathe into my chakras. I focus on letting go of the fear of losing my soulmate and focus my energy on my higher chakras.

I can feel the energy drain from my lower or base chakras, and when it does, I breathe light and power into my upper chakras. This allows me to cast out into the future, and I search for our shared energy.

I find us and smile as I watch Nikki and me continuing to train and fight together. We are in the gym in town and no longer in the compound, but I can see her strength and power have grown, and her light shines bright. We appear to be on the right path. I don't love the change in location as it puts the women in a position to become targets once Michael and Gabriel have a chance to heal, but it's better than the loss of them altogether.

I nod to myself as I take slower breaths and allow the image to fade. Next I cast out to Nikki. She opened our bond earlier this morning, and she isn't difficult to find as her anger hasn't waned. I find her energy in her rooms with Kate, and I focus on them as I breathe more power and energy into our bond.

Kate and Nikki have their duffle bags out and are quickly packing their items. Nik appears to have hers finished as she adds the last of the items from her closet and zips it closed. She moves to help her friend.

"Could you hear Aliyah and Isaiah's fight?" she asks softly. Their rooms are closer to Isaiah's than mine.

"Yeah." Kate looks sad. "Aliyah is so angry. It sounded like the guys forgot to mention to us that the Deveon warriors they are searching for could kill the humans they host if they are released."

"Yeah. I'm going to venture to say they didn't forget to mention shit. They just wanted us to agree to the bonds and help them release their mates. Doesn't look like they actually give a shit about us," Nikki replies angrily.

Kate stops and turns to Nikki. "Where exactly were you last night, Nik? You seem awfully angry on Aliyah's behalf," Kate tells her, almost playfully.

Nikki gives her friend a glare and finishes the packing. "I may have seduced Azrael and completed the second bond," she says with a wince.

Kate chokes on air and laughs. "May have? Jesus. I wish I could maybe seduce the guy I'm lusting after and gain superhuman powers."

I smile tightly, feeling the remarks cut as I watch them laugh about our bonds. I know it's just girl talk, but damn. I am completely unprepared for the pain of her next remark.

"It was nothing. Just another mistake in a long line of fuck ups on my part. Please let it go, Katie." Kate nods.

"Maybe it wasn't. Maybe they really are our destiny," Kate tells my soulmate, and Nikki turns away to wipe tears from her eyes.

"Maybe. But it doesn't matter much now. We go where Aliyah goes, and our girl is going home," Nikki tells her friend softly. Kate squeezes Nikki's shoulder, and they leave the room with their bags.

I close the bond and breathe into the pain in my chest at her careless remarks. I know it just comes from a place of anger, but I've been lost without this woman for thousands of years, and while I understand she is pissed about our deception, it also cuts deep to hear her callousness.

I quickly dress and grab my keys from the nightstand. I remind myself that she is hurt and that while I am pained to have lost the ground we made last night, I go where she goes.

Chapter Eleven

L etting Go
    Nikki

It's been two months since we left the Deveon compound, and there haven't been any attacks on us from the Anhelios. The three of us are staying at my place since Aliyah lost her apartment when she moved in with the guys and Kate was staying with me before we were so rudely kidnapped and held hostage for months.

The adjustment hasn't been the easiest. Aliyah is still angry and violent. She hasn't gotten the full hang of her new powers yet, and if I were guessing, I'd say she misses Isaiah and is just too damn stubborn to tell him.

"You do know I can fucking hear your thoughts, right?" Aliyah asks with her usual amount of anger as we spar at the Deveon's gym on First Street in Devil's Bend. I smile as I block her next two punches and sweep her leg out. She goes down hard, and I hear the air wheeze out as it escapes her lungs.

"Yep. But a girls gotta wax poetic from time to time, and the fact that you don't know how to turn off your gift isn't actually a *me problem*," I tell her as I wipe the sweat from my eyes and offer her a hand up.

"Nice, Nikki. Maybe if I consorted with the enemy from time to time, I would learn a few things too." She has a bitter edge to her voice, and she lets out a bit of her electrical surge when she takes my hand. I yelp and drop her back down onto the mat.

"Hey, not cool, babe. It is not my fault Isaiah did you wrong. I am your friend, and I've always got your back, but honestly, you are not winning any popularity contests with your anger issues and violent tendencies." I take a huge gulp from my water bottle and adjust my hair tie.

Aliyah laughs cruelly as she jumps to her feet and wipes her hands on her leggings. "Good to know. I'm actually not concerned with having you or anyone else here like me at the moment. I just want to train and take out as many of these assholes as we can. If we're destined to be Hunters, then I want to be the fucking best at it."

I nod at my friend and take a deep breath as I push out energy and power from my heart chakra and close her bond for her.

Aliyah smiles at me for the first time in weeks. "Did you just close my bond? That's amazing. Oh gods, thank you so much. It was actually driving me bat shit crazy feeling you and the guys' thoughts and feelings all the damn time. How did you do that?"

"Azrael taught me to close my bond last week. We've been working on energy work and patience in our training, and I just thought maybe I could do it for you. It worked I guess," I tell her as she hugs me.

"I'm so sorry for being so damn unbearable lately. You're not wrong." Aliayh lowers her voice and looks around the gym before continuing. "I do miss Isaiah. Well, not the asshole who wanted to let me die to get his fated mate back, but the guy I was falling in love with. The one who treated me like I mattered to him and that he didn't want to exist without me. I know that isn't who he really is, and I know it's making me a bitter bitch, but I can't seem to stop myself. Add in the impossible annoyance of not being able to stop myself from hearing you and Azrael and Rafa all the damn time, but unfortunately not the only man I do somehow want to hear. I've been a bit off my game."

I hug my friend back. "I'm not going to say it's ok because you really have been an asshole lately, but I do forgive you."

"Maybe with the bond closed, I could try working with the guys. I could use the help training with Rafa, and Azrael is really talented with the energy work ..." Her voice trails off, and I smile.

"I haven't heard anything about Isaiah. If you were wondering," I tell her, and she smiles back sadly.

"It doesn't matter. Whatever we could have been is gone now," she says as she turns away. "How are things between you and Az?"

"The same. We're done. I told you the bonding was a mistake, and it wouldn't matter anyway with you and Isaiah done ..."

"It's so strange that we need to complete the bonds in order for you to ... Are we sure that's a real thing? Maybe the guys are wrong and you or Kate could still bond with them and transition or whatever ..."

I shake my head."I mean, do you hear yourself? First, I don't want to bond with Azrael and potentially cease to exist. Fuck that. And secondly, we're doing our best to be Hunters and help their cause to save humanity. I don't think it's necessary to die for a mission we didn't sign up for. I'm just saying."

"Ok. If you're sure. I know how intense the bonds can be. I don't want you to suffer just because Isaiah and I are finished." She swallows hard, and I find myself unbelievably grateful that I didn't have a chance to fall in love with my demon before everything came to a screeching halt.

I shake my head again. "Girl, I don't know how else to tell you this. I don't want to share my body with a warrior who is in love with Azrael. That's just fucking creepy."

Aliyah laughs, "I know, right? Still, he is really fucking hot."

I smile sadly. "I am well aware. And yet somehow I manage not to attack him sexually on a daily basis. The struggle is real."

Aliyah snorts. "I need to talk to you and Kate about something important."

Kate bounces into the room with a tray of iced coffees and a smile that relays just how well her training session with Rafa went. I look at Aliyah, and she rolls her eyes. I guess we'll deal with Kate's blossoming obsession with Rafa when we have to.

We each take a coffee, and Kate smiles at Aliyah. "What's up, Queenie?" she asks, and I cover a laugh with a cough designed to hide my amusement.

"Just, no," Aliyah responds, and Kate smirks.

"I want to talk about the Archangel removal plans," she says quietly, and Kate and I both stand up a bit straighter. "I think the missions are going well."

"We have a 90% success rate," I tell them, and both girls nod approvingly. For the past several weeks, we have been tracking archangels to the bars and clubs in the area and systematically taking them out. It has been going perfectly to plan, and we have surpassed our goal of removing the assholes, I mean, Anhelios that we were originally hunting before our abduction.

"I'm feeling an increase in power. I was thinking that perhaps we're absorbing their power somehow? Is there any way to ask the guys if this is possible without letting them know about our nightly ritual?" Aliyah asks

I smile thoughtfully. "Humm, seems like a job for Kate."

"Perhaps you can mention it to Rafa in your next session without letting on that it's us, that we're the ones killing archangels and absorbing their power," Aliyah says without a trace of irony.

"I can do that. But I have to tell you guys that this is starting to get really fucking dark."

Aliyah turns to Kate and nods. "Yes. It is. That's kind of the fucking point, right? Or are we here to coddle these motherfuckers while they hunt down human women and then breed them to essentially wipe out the human race?"

Kate backs away with her hands in the air. "I'm not saying I disagree. The last time I checked, I was right there with you ladies tracking and killing. But I am saying maybe we need to take a minute to check in when what we're doing is so dark. We don't want the literal demons who are training us to know about it. I'm just saying ..."

Aliyah nods. "Ok. Point taken. And for the record, it's not that we don't want the Deveons to know what we are doing because they will disapprove of our motives. I really don't think that will be a problem.

It's more that they are a bit over protective, and I'm afraid they will see this as painting a target on our backs."

Kate nods. "Thats the fucking truth. Still I'm concerned about the power increase. Do you think the guys can feel it too?"

I shake my head. "If they can, then they are excellent actors. I don't feel anything through the bonds."

Aliyah nods. "True, but they are much more skilled at hiding their emotions than we are."

Kate looks thoughtful. "Do you think it's possible the Anhelios can feel the increase in power?"

"I haven't heard or felt anything about them through the bonds, but how long do you think the healing process actually takes?" I ask.

Aliyah smiles tightly. "I had that dream walk with Michael months ago, and I know he wasn't healed then. It's definitely possible he is now." Aliyah turns to me. "Can you slip it into the conversation with Azrael the next time you train?"

I look at my friend and notice how tired she looks. I'm not sure how much longer she can keep up the late night hunts. The anger and violence must be eating her up inside.

I frown. "Maybe it's time to tell the guys what we've been up to. I don't know if this is the best idea ..."

"Soon. Let's just take out the last few leads, and then we'll tell the guys. I just need to gain a little more power." Aliyah trails off.

"Ok. Kate, talk to Rafa about the power increase, discreetly, and I'll ask Azrael tomorrow about the timeline on the Anhelios healing. But Aliyah, next week we need to have a sit down with the Deveons and fill them in on the archangels genocide mission and our part in their disappearances, because I can guarentee that it hasn't gone unnoticed by the remaining Anhelios."

The others nod in agreement, and I smile, confident in our decision.

If only we hadn't been so sure that we had all this under control. If only we had agreed to tell the guys sooner. If only we had the ability to see into the future. Unfortunately, crystal balls are just pretend, right?

Chapter Twelve

Excursions
Azrael

I sip my coffee and grip the steering wheel as I watch Nikki, Aliyah, and Kate take on a literal gang of well-trained Archangels in a dark parking lot on the edge of town. I am parked in the shadows of a side street watching and waiting while I witness the chosen Hunters and my mate fight off men twice their size. My heart rate increases, and I subconsciously reach for the door handle.

"Give them a chance, Az." Rafa tells me without looking away from the scene.

I sigh and reach for my coffee again. "It's just hard to watch them doing this shit, night after night, and doing nothing to help."

Rafa snorts quietly from his place in the passenger's seat. "Right. Are you sure it's that you want to help, and not that you're afraid one of these bastards will kill your girl before you have a chance to complete the broken bonds?" He doesn't breakhis laser focus on the women we train and protect.

I shake my head. "Not a chance of completing the bonds now. Nik knows the score, and she's not interested in becoming a casualty of the gods' pettiness when Nyx is finally released."

"Gods, these women are so convinced they are going to be casualties of our mates. Does no one here actually remember the oaths we took to save humanity? It's tiresome the way you and Isaiah just step out of the picture because your women tell you they are done with you." Rafa shakes his head and tosses a handful of popcorn into his mouth as Aliyah drop kicks several of the men, and Nikki places a knife through their hearts while they are down.

The archangels fade from existence as their life force is drained. It is actually quite impressive to watch. I stare at the scene unfolding in front of me as Kate jumps onto the back of a man who is attacking Aliyah and stabs her knife into his neck.

"Isaiah and I are not just stepping back. Aliyah rejected him and the bonds. He is suffering the loss of another attempt, and honestly, our time is running out. He will lose his mind to the pain of her rejection. It is only a matter of time. I spoke with him earlier, and he is ready to return to Deveon before he loses his ability to reason and does something unthinkable."

Rafa nods and frowns. "He's not wrong. Isaiah running around the human dimension without his sanity isn't an option, especially with an impending apocalypse. It is only a matter of time before Gabriel and Michael heal and return to fuck our shit up." Rafa finishes the bag of popcorn and dumps the crumbs into his mouth. "This is ridiculous. You want Nikki. You began the bonds. So Isaiah and Aliyah have broken their fated bonds again. What is stopping you from taking up where they left off and releasing Nyx from her imprisonment? I don't even fucking want to be bonded, and I think you're both idiots."

I shrug. "Perhaps. And yet Aliyah, Nyx, and Keyra they are Deveon Warriors and queens. No one tells them what to do. Aliyah has chosen, and Nyx is following. I can do nothing if my mate denounces our bonds as well. Be patient Rafa. The universe is vast and just. When it is time for our mates to return, then they will. Nothing is forever." I watch Aliyah rise from the ground and stomp a man twice her size. My heart soars as Nikki tosses her a knife, and Aliyah finishes him off.

"Perhaps, my friend. But I'm not sure we'll have a world for our mates to return to if we don't do something soon. They are getting much better." Rafa says with a nod towards the women we are sworn to protect.

"Yes, they are."

The fight we have been watching is over, and Aliyah, Nikki, and Kate brush themselves off and head to their car to go back to their apartment.

"They have been hiding their hunting sessions from us, and while I find it slightly amusing that they think they can pull one over on us, I'm also pretty concerned about their nocturnal activities."

"It was a bold move. Impressive." Rafa replies as he watches them leave the parking lot. "Honestly, I've had my doubts that they were more than Hunters. A part of me was convinced that Isaiah and you were so desperate to have your mates back that you were seeing warriors where there were only humans ..." Rafa's voice trails off.

"And now?"

"And now I think we may actually have a chance at saving the humans. And as much as the thought of being bonded without a choice in who I'm spending eternity with is terrifying, I think the two of you need to get your heads out of your asses and complete the bonds so we have our powers and our bonds in place in time to destroy the Anhelios."

I stare at Rafa in shock. "Seriously? I thought you were dead set against completing the bonds with Keyra." I tell him, confused at this change in his well-known opinion on the bonds and bound powers.

Rafa watches the tail lights of the women's car as they disappear around the corner. There is a new found respect there. "I'm not dead set against bonding with Keyra." His voice sounds tired. "Kate is a cool chick, and increasing our powers is obviously a necessity. Gods, I'm not a monster. I want to save humanity and all that shit. I just don't feel the pull, man. This is a forever thing, and Kate is beautiful and sweet, but my soul doesn't gravitate to her, you know?"

"I don't actually understand. Nikki is it for me. As soon as I saw her, I wanted her for eternity."

Rafa nods. "Maybe that will come after the first bond. If Kate is Keyra, she has to be my mate right?" he asks me, his eyes still following the car long after the girls have gone.

"I don't know, man. The universe is fucking vast. Maybe we are wrong, and there's another mate for you out there somewhere." My voice trails off because we both know if there is someone else for Rafa, then finding her before our time runs out seems impossible.

"Maybe," he says, distractedly. "They really are impressive."

I nod as I put the keys in the ignition and follow the women home.

• • • •

"Azrael!"

I can hear her cry for help across several dimensions. Nikki. Her cries are followed by a plea from Aliyah. *Hey, a little help would be great. In the middle of an ambush by the Anhelios at Club Repent.*

My heart stills in my chest as I breath through my nose and out through my mouth. Trying to release energy from my lower chakras—fear, pain, and anger at the desperation in her cry and focus on finding her. We are too far away from Aliyah, Nikki, and Kate to be of any help to them.

Isaiah has returned to Deveon, worn down from the rejection and Aliyah's increase in power, which, after the rejection, only seems to drain him.

Devon is a vast dimension, and while we can teleport, it will take longer than I fear we have. Isaiah has returned to demon form here, and while he thrashes and screams in response to the cries he feels through his broken bonds, he would be of little help to us.

I try to focus my energy on making a bubble of calmness around Rafa and me. I focus on the stillness around me and push energy to my third eye to search for my mate. I find her energy pulsing in an old Evangelist Church several towns over from Devil's Bend in the human world.

Nikki's energy glows purple. It is usually a softer lavender, but tonight it glows a deep amethyst, and I am struck by the power surrounding it. She is pulling energy either from another fight or from beings more powerful than she is.

I don't have the time needed to search for what—or who—they are up against. We are too far away from them. I had hoped they would be safe while we pleaded with Isaiah to fight his insanity in hopes of bringing him back to the human world, but we didn't have the option of waiting any longer.

Rafa and I exchange looks. "We cannot take him with us," I tell Rafa.

He nods, and we teleport out of Deveon and into the old church. We move quickly, but time moves differently across dimensions, and the moments it took us to get here have been hours in this dimension.

War cries emit from our mouths as we dive into the battle. Without a second thought, Rafa and I release our wings and circle the huge warehouse from above. It is absolute chaos, and there is blood everywhere. Hundreds of archangels lay sprawled across the space, and anger tears through me as I focus all my energy on destroying anything in the way of my Queen, my mate, and our friend.

I see a flash of white and gold, and catch sight of Margot, an Anhelio I remember well from our long battles and even longer time sharing this world. Her golden blond hair flies free behind her as she stalks my mate, moving faster than Nikki's human form can track. I see red and fly towards them, ready to end her immortal existence.

"Et, et, eh. No interrupting the fun, old friend." Angelica, a bronze-skinned beauty with dark hair and eyes, stands tall and gorgeous, her face twisted in a cruel smirk as she steps between me and my intended target.

"Do not interfere, Angelica. I will have no regrets slicing your head from your body if you do not remove yourself now," I tell her, and her eyes darken slightly as she tilts her head to the side, as if examining an interesting bug.

"Are you desperate to save your precious queen? Or is it something more?" Her perception is sharper than I remember.

"I didn't see it before. I suppose I was too focused on this human version of Aliyah and Isaiah's obsession with her. But, make no mistakes, I see it now. You've found your mate as well, haven't you, Azrael?" Angelica continues to speak, ignoring the fact that I haven't responded and am currently surveying the room to find my mate.

"Is it the curvy blond we had in our dungeons for months torturing and training?" She watches me, and then when she sees what she is looking for, she throws her head back and laughs. "No? The other one then, the dark haired beauty with the foul mouth? Is that Nyx's host? Interesting. Gabriel had them both for months, you know. I wonder what else he had the human whores doing for him. He does love to taste the flesh, as they say."

Her words cut off as I plunge my sword into her shoulder.

"Touche. You had better hurry then, brother. Broken bonds do nothing to fight against us," Angelica tells me as I pull my sword from her shoulder and prepare to remove her head.

I swing out and slice through the air. Looking around, I see nothing, but I feel the flap of her powerful wings and then hear her voice ring out from above. "Time is running out. Your little Hunters may have ruined our breeding experiment, but we have an apocalypse to render. Don't worry, Azrael. War is coming."

I shake off the impending doom and look around for my mate. She and Margot have disappeared, and I lift my wings to take flight, circling from above and joining Rafa in picking off the archangels.

Shots ring out, and I screech in anger as I watch the last of the archangels flee out the doors. It is silent now. Aliyah makes her way to the middle of the warehouse.

"You called?" Rafa quips.

She smiles. "I did. Thank you for the assistance. It wasn't looking great for us for a moment there." She rips off a part of her shirt to wrap her wounded arm.

I search for Nikki and shudder as I watch her limp across the warehouse covered in blood. I can smell her blood and know she has a knife wound in her leg and cuts across her arms and chest. My anger is palpable as I turn to Aliyah.

"You know if you completed the bonding, you wouldn't need the help. We would just be back-up to you destroying whatever evil stands in your way."

She turns to stare at me. "You can't be fucking serious. Angelica just said the same damn thing to me before she attempted to end me. Everyone wants Isaiah and me to complete the fucking bonds so damn badly, but I don't see Isaiah actually bothering to help keep me alive." She spits the words out, frustration clear in her voice.

"Actually, I haven't seen Isaiah in months, so you can stop the guilt trips and quest for your precious queen. It's fucking over. Isaiah finally moved on, and now so can I. He didn't come. He doesn't give a shit if I live or die. Just let it go, Az."

With tears in her eyes, she turns to leave with Nikki and Kate flanking her. I am so angry I almost let her go. My anger outweighs my reasoning and sense of duty. As the adrenaline drains away, Rafa steps forward and calls out to their retreating forms

"Aliyah, wait. We need to tell you something."

Aliyah stops mid-stride. Nikki and Kate turn with her, almost as if the three of them are one now. My heart hurts as Nikki's eyes come to mine, and I see the loss there. And the hope.

I have the gift of sight. I can cast my energy and see the future, but even I can't see what this life holds for the six of us. If I could, I would have grabbed my mate and fled from that warehouse. Hell, even this damn dimension. But I didn't. None of us knew what would happen next.

Chapter Thirteen

Acceptance
Nikki

Isaiah has lost his mind and returned to Deveon. That is the jist of it.

After Azrael and Rafa responded to our cries for help at the Anhelio ambush, we returned with them to the Deveon compound, and they told us the truth about Isaiah's whereabouts and why he wasn't able to help us.

My mind is stuck on the details of the bonds that Azrael just let slip. Six bonds. Trust. Love. Acceptance. Lust. Desire. Sacrifice. No particular order. Every relationship is different, and the order is never the same, not even for the same couple. They come as your bond evolves. None of us know which bonds the others have completed. Not even the gods are privy to that information.

Aliyah and Isaiah completed five with Sacrifice being the second to last. If they complete their bonds, Love will be the final one. Azrael and I completed two. Three bonds, and powers are increased. Four bonds, and the commitment is sealed. Five bonds, and gifts are exchanged. Six bonds, and we all gain power while the Deveon Warrior is released.

Aliyah's electricity. Isaiah's ability to feel empathy. Those are the gifts. Azraels patience and sight ... would I have those powers if we completed two more bonds? I shake the thoughts away and focus on the discussion my friends are immersed in.

"Are you playing me, Rafa? Is this some kind of sick joke to get me to complete the bonding with Isaiah?"

"I wish that were possible, Aliyah. It's just not an option any longer," Azrael says sadly.

"Wait. I can't complete the bonding with Isaiah any longer? It's over?" Yes, it's over. Isaiah isn't in human or even Anhelio form now. He has been driven back to his full Deveon form. He is a demon burning in hell for eternity."

"Can you bring him back? Once I die and the bonds release him, can you bring him back?"

"We don't know. Isaiah doesn't want to come back. He doesn't want to continue to track you and plead with you to accept him. He has accepted your rejection. He doesn't wish to fight for the bond any longer. Isaiah feels that you have been clear in no longer wanting him as your mate. He has released you. In doing so, he cannot leave Deveon. So, he is stuck," Azrael explains.

"Wait. He is in demon form and in hell for eternity because I rejected him? Seriously? Can I go to Deveon and bring him back?"

Azrael and Rafa exchange glances. "No," Rafa answers, and Azrael looks away.

"Why are you lying to me, Rafa? Is there a way to go to Deveon and bring Isaiah back?"

"We can go, but he won't come back. We've tried, and he refuses. It's for the best. Isaiah isn't himself anymore. He cannot be trusted in this realm."

"So, Deveons can go but humans cannot?" Aliyah asks, trying to read in between the lines of what they are not telling us.

"Oh, you can go to Deveon. But humans cannot return. You would have to do the one thing you refuse to do. You would have to shed your human form in order to save him and bring him back," Azrael says, his voice hard with the belief that she will not make the sacrifice for his brother.

She nods. "Ok. Show me how to get there."

"No!" Kate cries out.

"No fucking way," I announce angrily. "Are you fucking insane, Aliyah? You will die, and the Queen of the Damned will take your body. Not to mention you'll be bonding with a literal demon in hell.

You will have to make love to a monster to get Isaiah back. No. Absolutely not."

"I would be a monster if I refused to do this, Nik. Isaiah is my soul mate. He exists for me. I have to do this for him." She says this as if she knows this is true, down to the last fiber of her being. As if this is her destiny.

Aliyah focuses her energy and brings up a golden ball of light. I watch as she puts everything she has into this energy form, and it grows in front of us.

I step forward. I'm not exactly sure why, maybe I mean to stop her, or perhaps I'm just drawn to the light, but just as my foot hits the floor in front of me, Azrael steps forward and wraps his arms around me, drawing me back and into his chest.

My body instantly relaxes into his, and I allow myself to sink into his warmth. I close my eyes and breathe in his scent. It's just for a moment, but when I reopen my eyes, Aliyah is gone. And so is the golden doorway.

• • • •

Weeks pass with no word from Aliyah and Isaiah. It's a hard adjustment. Azrael and Rafa invited us to stay with them while Aliyah was gone, and we accepted. It's a hard truth to acknowledge, but they may never return.

The days pass slowly. We train and heal from the ambush. Azrael went to the apartment and packed our things while we were in weapons training with Rafa. We haven't made any moves to continue with our hunting. We haven't done much of anything.

Kate and I are in the sauna after an especially jarring training session when she brings up our mission for the first time since Aliyah left for Deveon.

"What are you thinking, Nik?" she asks, her eyes closed and head tipped back. Her voice is casual. She could be asking what I want to make for dinner or which movie we should watch tonight. I know she isn't.

"I think we succeeded in destroying the Anhelios breeding program. I think we hurt their plans, and they are regrouping. I think that the only thing keeping the Anhelios from raging war down on us and the human race is the fact that Michael and Gabriel are still fucking healing and that Aliyah and Isaiah had better bond and get released really fucking fast, or you and I are going to have to step up and get bonded." I breathe in the hot air and attempt to remain calm.

Kate opens her eyes and glances my way. "I think it's time to have a truth talk with Azrael and Rafa."

"What if she doesn't come back, Kate?" Tears fill my eyes for the first time in weeks. "What if all of this savior and Chosen One shit is all on us now?"

Kate smiles tightly and reaches out to hug me. "I hate to tell you this, my friend. But I think we've been leaning a little too hard on Aliyah as the Chosen One. This," she says, gesturing around us, "is on all of us. I don't want to cease to be when Keyra is released, but what fucking difference will that make if humanity is erased? Does my existence mean more than the whole of the human race?"

I hold on tighter to my friend and laugh softly. "No?" Kate's shoulders shake with her laughter as she pulls away and leads me out of the sauna and into the gym. "We may be all that's left of the chosen prophecy, and if that's the case, I choose you. I choose Rafa. I choose the survival of humanity. What do you choose, Nik?"

I blow out a breath and release the fear and anxiety that has been haunting me since Aliyah stepped into hell.

"I choose you, too. I choose Az, and I choose humanity."

Kate squeezes my hands as I feel a bond click into place. My eyes widen, and I can hear Azrael's voice in my head. *Nice, darling. That felt like the acceptance bond clicking into place. Does that mean what I think it means?*

I smile and release Kate's hands.

That I'm ready to accept my place in the prophecy. That I accept you. That's great, babe. But that's not exactly what I was hoping for.

I smile wickedly and peek over at Kate who is busy grabbing a towel to wipe off the sweat from our sauna.

Really, Az? And what were you hoping the acceptance bond meant?

I choke on air as I get an image of Azrael sliding his very large cock into me. We're in his bed, and it looks like later tonight if I had to guess.

I was hoping for the moment I get back from grabbing all this shit, darling. Hoping you can take that sweet ass upstairs and wait for me to get home.

I smile and shoot Azrael an image of me climbing bare-ass naked into his bed and letting my knees fall open. I laugh as I hear him groan over our bond.

Be there in 20 minutes. Don't you dare fucking move from that bed.

Kate laughs as she turns from the mirrors and drops her towel into a dirty bin. "Wow. So you two don't even have to be in the same room to bond or, like, communicate?" she asks in awe.

I laugh. "Something like that. Az is big on using the telepathy bond for visuals. If you know what I mean."

Kate throws her head back and laughs "Wow. Ok. He seems so serious and stoic. I honestly never would have guessed."

"I know, right? He's full of surprises. What about Rafa? You said you choose him. Did a bond slide into place for you?"

Kate shakes her head. "I'm pretty sure that only works if your mate feels what you feel. Rafa doesn't want me like that, but I'm hoping if the fate of the world hangs in the balance, he will accept me too."

I watch my friend with concern. "Are you sure Kate? Maybe there is another way?"

Kate shakes her head. "We'll see. But regardless, we're doing this. I just have to figure out what he wants and offer it."

I open my mouth to argue with her reasoning when the whole room seems to shake violently. There is a slow rolling of reality, a loud *BOOM,* and then nothing but darkness.

Chapter Fourteen

Conversations with Gods
Nikki

One minute I was standing in the Deveons' compound gym with Kate, and the next, there was some sort of cosmic boom. It was unbelievably loud, and the world seemed to roll for a moment, pulsing in and out of existence. And then there was utter darkness. I'm not sure how long the darkness lasted, but the next thing I knew, I was waking up in a literal hell dimension.

Now I'm human, so I have never actually been to a hell dimension before, but seeing how I had been standing in a normal gym in a normal town in Devil's Bend, Arizona, one minute and the next in a world with purple and gray skies, literal walls of fire, and lava rushing beneath the rock I am currently perched on, I'd say this is pretty much anyone's version of hell.

I'm not saying it isn't strikingly beautiful and oddly familiar to me. I'm just saying it is freaky as fuck, and I want out as soon as humanly possible.

Speaking of getting the fuck out of this weird hell dimension, what the actual fuck am I doing here? Did I die? And if so, why would I have ended up in hell? It isn't like I was a bad person. I wasn't. I was a freaking Hunter for God's sake. I was literally one of the chosen ones destined to save humanity, or so I had been told by three sexy-as-hell demons who were trying to save humanity and kick some serious angel ass in the process.

So, it stands to reason that I am not dead. I just got sucked into some sort of hell dimension.

Just as I am sorting out all this crazy ass bullshit in my head, I hear another loud boom followed by screeching laughter. And when I say screeching, I mean hands over my ears, head throbbing with an oncoming migraine sort of screeching, followed by the sky parting above me and three beings dropping down onto the rocks of hell I am currently residing on.

The ground beneath me is really just a series of rocks split every foot or so by deep crevices. Beneath the crevices is quickly flowing lava. It is terribly hot here. Hotter than August in the desert, and dry. I watch as the beings drop a good twenty feet from me and focus their attention on me. It is painful to look upon them. They are unbelievably beautiful. I had thought that Azrael, Rafa, and Isaiah were by far the most attractive beings I had ever met, but these three absolutely put our guys to shame.

The first to speak is a breathtakingly beautiful god with long dark hair, bronze skin, and deep eyes so dark they appear black. She has incredibly exquisite features, full red lips, and a striking figure clad in a gold dress.

"Nyx. So lovely to see you, my child. I'm terribly sorry it is under such dire circumstances," she tells me in a monotone that sounds anything but sorry.

I watch her wearily. "I'm afraid you have the wrong person. My name is Nikki, and I'm fairly certain this is a huge misunderstanding." I look between the three beings before me that I can only assume are gods.

The woman standing next to the god who addressed me throws back her head and laughs. I wince in pain and edge backward away from them.

"Aw, look sister. Nyx doesn't know us. She appears terrified," says the god. She has long, wavy blond hair, crystal eyes. and a perfect face. She wears gold wide-legged pants and a black sleeveless tunic.

"I am not terrified. Just a bit concerned as to who you are and what I am doing here." I ignore the shiver of fear currently sliding down my spine.

"Of course you would be confused in this silly human shell," the last of the gods informs me, laughing. He is gorgeous with dark hair, a sharply cut jaw, full lips, and jewel-like orbs for eyes. He wears black dress pants and a black silk shirt with a gold tie.

"We are the sibling gods—Enhil, Ishtar, and Enki. We are celestial beings who inherited the Earth at the beginning of your time," the female who first addressed me says.

I stare at the gods in confusion.

The one who is speaking to me sighs. "I am Ishtar, the youngest sibling. This," she says, gesturing to the woman standing to her left, "is Enhil, my sister, and this," she says, gesturing to her right, "is Enki. We have ruled this realm since before life here was created. In fact, we created you, Nyx. Your name literally means Night or the goddess of night. You were an Anhelio when we created you."

I stare at these beings and wonder if I have lost my damn mind.

The male god, Enki smiles tightly at me. "No, I assure you, you are quite sane."

I swallow my fear and try desperately to block my thoughts. The youngest god, Ishtar, laughs, a tinkling sound this time, and I wonder if they can control how they sound and appear to us.

"Silly child. You cannot block us from reading your thoughts. You are just a human. Humans are unbearably inferior."

"Ah, but that is why you are here, Nyx. We are challenging you. This is your first challenge in a series of trials to escape from hell and claim your Deveon form," Enki tells me as he watches my reaction.

"I'm sorry. Did you just say Deveon form?" I ask in wonder.

"Ah yes, quite distasteful, but you did choose to follow Aliyah and attempted to destroy our creations, the other Anhelios, and their offspring, the archangels. You had to be punished," Enki says.

Ishtar claps her hands together. "Tell her the story of Good versus Evil and her fall from grace," she demands excitedly.

Enhil sighs. "Very well, sister. In the beginning, the Earth was given to the three of us to do as we choose. We were to be the true gods of this realm. As celestial beings, we were sent to Earth to create a pantheon of twelve Anhelios, or what humans would later refer to as angels. Six male and six female Anhelios would rule over the Earth in our place. They were tasked with creating and nurturing a race of beings destined to be enslaved."

Ishtar laughs and claps her hands again. "Humans, they created humans!" she calls in a sing-song voice.

Enhil smiles. "Yes. Our early beings were ruled by the Anhelios. If I remember correctly, the Anhelios did not mate with one another in those days," she says, nodding to Enki.

He smiles. "We created the Anhelios in our likeness, god-like and powerful, all knowing in many ways. They were painfully beautiful to the humans we created later. They saw glowing skin covering strong muscular bodies, rich, vibrant hair, jewel eyes, and claw-like nails. They had cruel mouths twisted into condescending smirks," Enki remembers.

Enhil smiles. "Yes, they moved about the Earth naked in those days, with only their wings to cover them if they chose. To one another, they varied in beauty so pure it could be mistaken as ugliness. I loved the Anhelios in those days. They were so raw and beautiful. They worshiped us as we should be worshiped and believed that they had been created by a trio of gods so powerful they could only be what they called true beings."

Ishtar frowns. "Yes, but then they rebelled. We had been painfully wrong; our beautiful creation and their slaves turned on us."

Enhil sighs. "Good and evil were not concepts we thought about in those days. Our original creations, the Anhelios, were beings who thrived on purity. They did not believe in base instincts or acts, and only engaged in the mating ritual to produce a new race of beings. Simple beings who could not reproduce as they lacked the knowledge or desire to do so. They were what we came to call humans. They were created as a slave race to build this new world and were of little consequence to us or our Anhelios then."

Ishtar shakes her head and sighs. "But all of that changed eventually?"

"Yes. Over millennia, their thoughts about humans changed. Humans had become fascinating to many of them," Enhil says.

"But why? All this trouble for nothing but a race of beings created simply to work?" Ishtar says, disgusted.

"They had their own beauty; while they were innocent and childlike, they were evolving. They could feel and experience emotion on a level we and our Anhelios were incapable of. They loved and desired. They felt passion and resentment. They could be cruel and jealous like us and our Anhelios, yet they would learn from their mistakes and become better versions of themselves," Enhil reminds her sister.

She nods. "Ah yes. And then over time, the twelve Anhelios split into two separate views and perspectives. There became a great divide in their race, with half of them desiring to be more human. To free them from their servitude and walk among them. To experience life with them and to evolve with them."

"The other half of their race wanted to destroy the human child-like wonder. They tried to keep them as enslaved people and not allow them to experience their own lives and feelings. Those Anhelios who wanted to destroy humans thought their feelings and base instincts were disgusting and unworthy of the shared blood in their veins," Enki says.

Enhil nods, acknowledging his words as she continues the story with Ishtar. "The six Anhelios who wanted to save the humans were Aliyah, the great Angelic warrior; her lover, Isaiah; his brother, Rafa; Keyra, Aliyah's friend; Nyx, you little human; and Azrael, your lover. You became a chosen family who would fight against others to protect humans. In the early days, we had given you a patch of land to create life and a garden. The humans lived within this garden and worked the land, expanding it across the barren earth and making a habitat worth returning for."

Enki laughs. "And then you stupid Anhelios decided to reward them for their hard work by giving them the gift of knowledge and the ability to reproduce. What a terrible decision and the first in a long line of decisions that spit in the face of all we had given you."

Enhil continues the story, "The six Anhelios who despised the humans were Michael, Gabriel, Lutheran, Eliana, Margot, and Angelica. They chose to descend upon the humans and mate with them. Forcing a new race of beings to come into existence, stronger and more powerful with gifts that were unknown to us at the time. They are known as archangels or half breeds."

Enki smiles cruelly. "So, this act of genocide came after the time of human enlightenment and angered the Anhelios who respected humans. You were enraged by their objectification and wanted revenge. It forced a great divide in our little experiment."

Ishtar claps her hands together. "And so you fought!" she exclaims, excited to get to the action of the story.

Enhil smiles at Ishtar. "The great divide forced a battle known as The War of the Winged Beasts. You fought one another and struck each other down. There was bloodshed and loss, and when it was over, most of the humans and archangels were dead. They had paid the price for the Anhelios' selfishness and anger."

Ishtar smiles. "Ah yes. I remember; we returned in a fit of rage to strike them all down. Those of you who had helped the humans were considered Fallen and renamed the Deveons. They were forced into Deveon, a hell dimension where they were to live in solitude until they could escape and assimilate with the humans."

Enki nods. "The Anhelios who had tried to destroy the humans were stripped of their powers and forced to live among them. The ultimate insult, if I do say so myself."

Enhil continues, "And the archangels who survived the battle were forced to take human form, to reincarnate over and over again without the knowledge or memories of what they once were. These half-breeds were known as Hunters."

I swallow hard as all three sets of gods' eyes focus on me.

Ishtar claps her hands again in delight. "That's you, Nyx. And when the Hunters were reborn, you could sense the Anhelios, archangels, and Deveons. You would retain some powers while in human form. You could hunt and bond with Anhelios or Deveons, but you would not remember your previous lives."

"Exactly, Ishtar. The Hunters were essentially the balance for humanity. If properly trained, the Hunters would eventually kill all the archangels and bring about salvation for the Fallen. Or the end to the Deveons' kind and a new reign of servitude under the dominance of the Anhelios." Enki laughs and shrugs. "Either way, an exacting punishment for entitled lower beings."

Enhil continues the story, "When the Deveons had angered us and we sentenced their kind to Deveon, we did not allow the three who offended us the most to stay with their family. Aliyah and her warriors, Nyx and Keyra, were forced into human form as Hunters."

Enki laughs harshly. "Anhelios and Deveons can bond with Hunters. To complete the bonds means to love them, mate them, experience pain and lust, and eventually trust them. There are six bonds, and with each completed bond, the Hunter regains more power, and the Anhelio or Deveon group they are bonding with regains more power. Once the bonding is complete, the Hunters would become who they once were, with all their memories and powers intact."

Ishtar laughs with Enki and Enhil. "It is a good origin story. Human mythology calls this Angels and Demons. The battle of Good versus Evil."

Enhil smiles. " Ah, but history is written by the victors, and in this case, the Anhelios became the Angels, and the Deveons became the Demons. Those who sought to destroy humanity became the ones who are worshiped by it."

Enki laughs again. "I adore a good origin story, especially one as dark and tragic as this."

I stare at the gods in confusion. "So I am Nyx, an Anhelio who fell from grace and was sentenced to become a Deveon and then forced into a human shell until I can bond with my chosen mate and regain my powers?"

Enhil laughs and smiles at me cruelly. "Yes. You have been reincarnated hundreds of times, Nyx. Aliyah has failed to accept her mate in each of those reincarnations, and so you were out of the game so to speak."

Ishtar interrupts her sister. "But now, Aliyah and Isaiah have completed the bonds, and you are back on the board. So, we challenge you to find a way out of this dimension. A task which cannot be done in human form." Ishtar giggles excitedly. "You will have to find a way to bring your chosen mate here and complete the bonding in order to escape this dimension."

Enki smiles. "The bonding, though, is not to be taken lightly. Once completed, you will become fated mates for all eternity. Isaiah has tried many times to complete the bonds with Aliyah and has failed every time. Until now. It was a perfect revenge."

"Now you must complete your destiny to help the Deveons save humanity. It cannot be done from here though, human. And you cannot return to your dimension until you have bonded and shed this human form."

I stare at the gods in horror.

Ishtar giggles happily. "Good luck, Deveon Warrior. You are going to need it."

With that, the gods vanish, and I am left alone, exhausted and desperate to find a way out of this mess.

Chapter Fifteen

Gone

A zrael

. . . .

"Az, you still with me, man?" Rafa asks as he continues to bench press the insane amount of weight he currently has stacked on the bar.

"Yep. I'm here. Just a little distracted. I'm good now. I got you." I shake the telepathic images Nikki just sent me of her climbing naked into my bed out of my head.

Not an easy feat since, to be honest, that was probably the hottest imagery of my life. Not saying her touching herself wasn't hot. Just that this was a damn written invitation that I have every intention of accepting.

"Sure, man. Just make sure whatever is more important takes a backseat if I start struggling here." He grits his teeth as he pushes more than 1000 pounds above his head.

"Nik just completed our third bond," I tell him casually.

"Damn. Don't you actually have to be involved for that to happen?" Rafa asks, a look of concern in his eyes at the idea we could bond without our knowledge or participation.

"Right? You look worried, man," I tell him, enjoying his discomfort.

"Nah. I just wasn't aware they could do that. Don't they need consent or something if they are going to be forcing bonds?" he responds as he swallows hard.

"Yes, you need consent, or at the very least participation, to form a bond. If we didn't, Isaiah and Aliyah would have released their bound bonds centuries ago." I smile at Rafa as he racks his weights.

"Thank the gods. Not saying I'm not happy for you though. Just not interested in getting non-consent bonded is all."

"Yes. Having the most powerful Deveons in the world connected to us and sharing their power and gifts is a gross violation of our rights man." I bite back my smile.

"Fuck off, dick. I'm just not sure I want the whole bound for eternity thing. I'm not comparing bonding with Kate or Keyra or whoever she is as non-consensual. I am just saying I'm glad to hear it's not possible to bond without deciding to do it."

I laugh. "I know man. You gotta come around though. We need our warriors back if we're going to save humanity. Honestly, I'm not even sure we have a choice in saving humanity. If we don't fight the Anhelios, they will take us out."

Rafa nods thoughtfully. "I get that. I do. And I'm a fan of humanity. The humans have been very giving. I have enjoyed their continued debauchery and open mindedness. I also genuinely like them and think they deserve to have their freedom to procreate or not. No judgments here," he says with a wink.

I groan at his ridiculous antics. "Look, I understand you like your options open. Maybe Keyra does too. Whatever. Maybe discuss that. But you gotta get on board here."

I am surprised when I see anger flash across his face. It's gone a moment later, but I'm certain I saw it.

"So, how exactly did your mate complete the third bond if you weren't there? Asking for a friend," he says, his good-natured smile returning.

I laugh. "I'm not entirely sure how that was possible. Normally it is a shared experience. Still, if it was the acceptance bond, then I had already accepted her millennia ago and have been waiting for her for thousands of years ... so yeah, there's that."

Rafa nods tightly. "So we can bond even if Alyiah and Isaiah are undecided, huh?"

"Looks like it. Although, the way Aliyah conjured the dimensional doorway and walked through without a backward glance, it doesn't look like they are undecided about their fate any longer."

"Right. Shit."

I clap Rafa on his shoulder. "Talk to Kate. You'll figure it out. I gotta go, man. I need to grab some shit for the girls from their apartment. I promised Nikki I would be home soon, and I'm already running late."

Rafa nods, and I don't wait for anything else as I tear out of the gym and head to the girls' apartment.

. . . .

I tried to contact Nikki to let her know I was running a few minutes behind as I was leaving their apartment, but she didn't respond. I'm hoping she just fell asleep waiting for me, and I can wake her up in fun, new ways when I get to the house.

Gods. Three bonds. With any luck, we'll complete the fourth bond tonight. I laugh at myself and groan inwardly. I'm really not sex obsessed. I think I'm actually more Nikki obsessed. It's been a long damn time since I let myself think of the possibility of having my partner and friend back. Nyx was once the other half of me, and having her ripped away was torture.

But she completed the acceptance bond. She is all in. Even knowing Nyx will be released and she may lose a part of herself in accepting her true goddess form, Nikki wants this. She wants me, and I am finally allowing myself to believe this is real. The bonds do tend to be tied to high emotional levels, and sex tends to bring those out.

I'm just trying to help save humanity. Right?

I take the stairs three at a time to get to the woman who just agreed to be mine. Again. For eternity.

Smiling like a dumbass, I let myself into my room, fully expecting to find Nik naked and asleep on my bed. She isn't there, and to be honest, it doesn't look like she ever was.

I frown as I survey the bedroom and head down the hall to her and Kate's rooms to see if she just got tired of waiting for me and went to her own bed.

Nothing.

Neither girl is here, and nothing is disturbed. They didn't take their clothes or toiletries. They didn't make their beds or pick up the towels in the bathroom. Absolutely nothing is different than it has been in the weeks since Aliyah left and they returned to the compound to stay with us.

What. The. Fuck?

· · · ·

It's been several hours since I came home to find Nikki missing. I've literally looked everywhere. She is gone. Kate is missing as well.

"It doesn't make sense that they would just take off and leave all of their shit. Maybe Kate, she's not tied to us the way Nik is now, but why not just tell us?" Rafa says as he watches me go through the video surveillance of the house.

"Maybe Nik changed her mind about us." I finally voice the one thing I've been thinking for the past few hours but have been too afraid to put out into the universe.

"No," Rafa says. "Not a chance. I see the way she looks at you. Even before the girls left with Aliyah. She wouldn't leave without a damn good reason, and with the acceptance bond, I don't think she'd leave you even if Aliyah changed her mind about Isaiah again. That woman loved you before we were damned as the Fallen, and she still does."

"You think?" I swallow my fears and focus on the images on the screen.

Rafa drops a hand on my shoulder and squeezes. "Yeah, man. I really do."

I pause on an image of the girls in the gym earlier today.

"That's fucking weird. Look. They're both in the gym here, and then just moments later, the gym is empty." I review the time stamp on the video.

"Did someone alter the surveillance?" Rafa asks as he watches over my shoulder.

"No. I don't think so. It looks clean." I check the footage again. "It's just so fucking weird. One minute, the girls are talking in the gym, and the next, they are just gone. Maybe the Anhelios?"

Rafa looks perplexed. "Maybe. I don't see how they could have done it though. I don't even see them walk out of view. They just vanish."

"I know. Maybe a false lure of some kind? Telling them we were in danger or that they had someone the girls care about?"

"Whatever they did, they will fucking pay for it. It's time to pay those fucking angels a visit again."

I turn off the monitors and head for the weapons room.

Chapter Sixteen

New Friends

Nikki/Nyx

Hell is interesting. I'm not saying it's comfortable—it's really not. Especially in human form. It's really fucking hot, and with the lava flowing beneath the rocks and the strange purple and grey sky, it never really changes. The moon and sun cycle I am used to doesn't appear to exist here. So there isn't a clear passing of time.

I awoke after my confrontation with the gods and decided to find water and shelter. It took hours to find a cave-like structure with a waterfall towards the back of the cave.

The lukewarm water feels amazing. It would have been nice to find cold stream water, but this will have to do. I try to reach Azrael telepathically. I am desperate to tell him what the gods have done, but they were honest in their assessment that I would not be able to reach him.

I have to assess the situation the way my demon lover would. The god's said, "I was back on the board." So Aliyah and Isaiah have completed their bonds, and now they are focused on forcing me out of their game. Interesting detail. So if that's the way the game is played, they appear to move one of their pieces at a time, and apparently it's my lucky day.

If this is Deveon, then this was the cage that Azrael, Rafa, and Isaiah were sentenced to until they could break free and make their way to the human dimension. Ok. If it took them centuries to find a way out of here even with all of their powers, then I have no chance of getting out without a little help.

I float on my back and allow the water to cool my skin as I contemplate this situation. I have to clear my mind and release any negative thoughts. This is difficult—my first instinct is to fight. To find something to hit.

Azrael is always preaching energy release and chakra cleansing as the first step in controlling one's power and emotions. Decision made, I roll over in the water and make my way to the edge of the pool. I lift myself out of the water and sit on the edge of the pool with my legs dangling.

"Hey," a voice says, and I turn to find a red-haired woman standing a few feet away from me. She is breathtakingly beautiful in the same way as the Deveons. I also feel a strong connection to her as soon as our eyes meet.

"Hi." I say with hesitation

She smiles reassuringly. "I don't want to frighten you. I'm Sasha."

"I'm Nikki—Nyx, I guess."

She smiles again. "I know. I'm Fallen too. You don't remember?" Her brow creases with concern.

"No. I actually have no memories of being Anhelio or Fallen for that matter."

Sasha nods. "Right. So you were reincarnated then?"

"Yes. I'm human so I can't transport or, you know, get out of Deveon."

"Same. I mean I'm not human, but I am stuck here. I'm waiting for one of the Fallen to return. It's prophesied that once Fallen, the Deveons would be sentenced to hell only to find their way out and find their bonded mates and save humanity. Soooo, I'm waiting for you. I guess."

"Um. I'm not sure how I can help. I'm not even sure if I can find a way out of here. The gods said this was a challenge, and I have to find my way to my mate ..."

Sasha smiles. "Well, if it helps, Azrael and Nyx were in the first few stages of the bonds when war broke out and we were all damned."

"That is what the guys said."

"You know them then?" she says, looking relieved.

"Yes. Az and I are bonding. Were bonding, before the gods snatched me away for this bullshit game of theirs. I'm actually not sure what we are now, if anything."

Sasha laughs softly. "Well, if you're anything like Nyx, then you will find that man. Not even the gods or well, hell, could stop the two of them. I've never known two people to be so in love. Not even Aliyah and Isaiah were as deeply in love as you and Az. Just saying."

"Ok. So how do you fit into the story then?"

Sasha throws her head back and laughs. "Damn. You're definitely Nyx." I smile tightly and wait for her to continue. "We weren't exactly friends, Nikki. Nyx was a lot. Opinionated. Highly motivated, straight forward, demanding. You have a lot of her in you. I'm an empath. Before the War of the Winged Beasts, I stayed away from the other Anhelios for the most part. Too many strong emotions can overwhelm me. Mostly I helped the gods to understand humans. My role did more damage than good, and when Aliyah approached me to join your band of angels seeking resistance I jumped at the chance to help right what I considered my wrongs."

"So you no longer consider your helping the gods as wrong?" I ask her. Sasha scrunches her nose thoughtfully. "I do. I want to help humans. I am committed to saving humanity. But I was sentenced to Deveon thousands of years ago, and while Isaiah, Rafa, and Azrael were able to escape this dimension hundreds of years ago, I've been here since before the sentencing."

"Why didn't you escape with the guys?"

Sasha sighs. "They believed I had died during the war. I was trapped in an alternate timeline while they were here and was only released to this dimension after they escaped. It's a lot. I know. I can help you though. I understand how the gods think. If we are going to get free of this place and help save humanity, then we need to work together."

I watch her thoughtfully. "What do you mean by an alternate timeline?"

"I'm actually not sure. But the way I understand it, time is not exactly linear. So while the guys were stuck here, in a prison so to speak, I was in the same dimension on a separate timeline, making it impossible for our paths to cross. Much like you were on earth being born over and over again while we were here."

"Huh. So when the guys escaped, you dropped into this timeline?"

Sasha wrinkles her nose again. "Sorta. More like once the guys escaped, the gods' hold was released, and the timelines blended into one."

I watch her for a moment. "Ok. I suppose that makes sense if the gods are consistent in keeping all the Fallen apart. They appear to only move one piece at a time, like a chess game. So, what do we do first?"

Sasha smiles. "First we ground and cleanse your chakras. Then we ask for guidance from a higher power."

I stare at her, and she laughs, "Let's sit at the edge of the water and concentrate on our breathing."

I nod as Sasha drops down next to me. "Once seated, we need to begin grounding our physical bodies. Did the guys teach you energy work?" "Azrael always taught deep breathing and visualization as a means for grounding." I take a deep cleansing breath and visualize my lungs expanding and collapsing.

"Good, let's try visualizing ourselves as a tree," Sasha suggests, and I imagine my lower body as the trunk and my head and arms as the branches. I visualize the roots dangling from my feet and then see them sinking deep into the earth.

"Good, now allow the roots to sink deeper and deeper into the earth, expanding and growing as they find purchase in the earth."

I do as she suggests, and I feel grounded and strong. Capable and sure.

Knowing this is a good sign, I take another deep breath in. Sasha nods and breathes in deeply and out completely.

"Now imagine sending any and all negative thoughts, feelings, and beliefs out of your body."

I visualize the negative energy, and then I send it down the length of my body and out through the roots. I imagine these thoughts as swirling, dark gray energy, and I envision it floating further and further away from me.

"Next, breathe in deeply and breathe out completely. Imagine bright golden light flowing down from the top of the cave and flowing down over you from the crown of your head to the tips of your toes."

I breathe in this beautiful golden light and envision it swirling down around my head and ears. I see it circling my eyes and flowing along my cheekbones and back behind my ears. I imagine this beautiful golden energy flowing into my throat and down into my chest. As I breathe in deeply and breath out completely, I imagine the golden light flowing down over my ribs and back around my organs as it flows deep into my belly and down into my pelvis.

The golden light dances and flows all around my body until it sinks deeper. The light flows down around my waist and my hips. Flowing and swirling as it flows down along the length of my legs and into my feet. The golden energy flows and swirls until it moves into each and every toe and then back up along my legs and thighs. Slowly swirling and moving around my waist and my hips until it reaches my tailbone where I release any excess energy.

"Ok. Good. Now I want you to focus on a rope of lightness and brightness dropping from your tailbone deep, deep into the earth. Imagine this rope sinking deeper and deeper and even deeper into the earth. Got it?"

I nod.

"Good. Imagine just letting go," she tells me.

I let go of any and all of the excess golden energy. Just breathing in deeply and breathing out completely. I sit like this for a long time. Just breathing. Fully grounded and somehow safe in a hell dimension I've never been in before.

I smile and send out thanks to the universe. To my mate and to my chosen family, the Deveons we once were and hopefully will be again soon. I sit at the edge of the pool and just let go.

Sometime later, I giggle.

"What's up?" Sasha asks as we sit in silence, our eyes closed and breathing deep and regular.

"I was just thinking about this popular children's movie. *Let it go* is the entire message behind the movie."

Sasha smiles. "And that's funny because?"

"I don't know. I suppose I, being a reincarnated demon warrior/fallen angel who is currently stuck in hell, am so far from a princess in a frozen realm and yet ..."

Sasha laughs. "Right. I got it. You're the exact opposite of this childhood ideal, and yet you're the same in a lot of ways."

I laugh. "Something like that. Good gods, Azrael would be so freaking proud of me! I actually do listen to him."

Sasha smiles at me. "You were always quick. It was letting others take the reins that you had a problem with. I believe the word for it now is strong-willed."

I laugh. "Ok, now what do we do after grounding and releasing work?"

"What would Azrael say?"

"Oh right, chakras. If Azrael were here with me, we would be working on cleansing our chakras."

"Good. So let's do that."

I bring my feet up to a crossed leg position and continue to do breath work as I focus my energy on my lowest chakra.

"Good. You need to cleanse your base chakras in order to open and breathe positive energy into your higher chakras."

I nod. This is how we were able to communicate telepathically and how I was able to close the telepathy bond for Aliyah after she rejected her bound bonds with Isaiah.

"My lowest chakra is my root chakra. Azrael would always say this was stability and truth."

"Good. Imagine the purifying golden light flowing through the base of your spine and around your legs. Next, envision a bright ruby red flowing around your lower body and into the base of your spine."

I breathe in stability, truth, and acceptance.

Smiling, I move up my body to my second chakra, the sacral chakra.

"Imagine the golden light flowing around your waist, hips, and belly button, releasing any sexual frustration and resentment you may have built up around your own sexuality, previous partners, or lack of interaction with your demon."

I smile as I imagine a brilliant rust orange flowing in and around me. I breathe in healing, acceptance, and release.

"Good. Next, concentrate on your third chakra or solar plexus, the area in your stomach and lower chest. This area represents self esteem, willpower, and personal responsibility."

I breathe in the golden light and imagine it flowing over my lower chest and swirling around my tummy. I then breathe in more golden light the color of bright yellow marigolds or poppies. I let the vibrant yellow move through me and around me.

"Now, taking a big breath, move golden light into your fourth chakra or heart area. This area governs healthy relationships and an imbalance can be represented by depression," she tells me softly.

I breathe in deeply and breath out completely imagining a vibrant emerald green flowing into my heart and chest cavity. While doing this, I think of Azeael and Kate. I envision Aliyah and Isaiah and Rafa back home. I see all of us happy, healthy, and whole. I hope for the best. And I send that wish out into the universe.

"Good. Nikki, you're doing great. Now, moving higher, envision your fifth chakra or throat chakra. This is the area in your throat which governs communication and voicing your own truth."

A tear slips down my cheek. This has been a big block for me for the majority of my life. My eyes fill with tears as I imagine cleansing golden light flowing down my throat and releasing the blockage there. Letting go of the hurt and inability to vocalize what I need versus what I anticipate others need from me. I take in a deep, deep breath and visualize bright blue energy flowing along my throat and healing me. The tears slip down my face as I process these powerful emotions.

Sasha hugs me. "Moving forward to your sixth chakra or third eye. Focusing your attention on the center of your forehead."

I lift my face and imagine the golden light flowing into me, cleansing my third eye and allowing my imagination, creativity, and intuition to flow freely as I breathe in a beautiful, deep amethyst purple flowing through me and around me.

Smiling Sasha nods her approval. "Now let's focus your energy on your seventh chakra or your crown. This is known for higher knowledge or connection to the divine."

I breathe the golden light in through the crown of my head and allow it to flow into my mind and around my head. I bring in a vibrant violet or purplish pink color, allowing it to flow into me and bring knowledge and truth.

Completing the grounding and energy work followed by chakra cleansing and opening, I allow the tears to roll down my face and flow freely. Sasha smiles at me reassuringly through her own tears.

"The release of energy in this place under these conditions is overwhelming, and while you may feel stronger and empowered in this moment, it's also normal to feel somehow smaller and completely aware of the vastness of the universe."

omehow that resonates with me on a level I didn't know was possible.

This acceptance of my own humanity opens something inside of me and allows me to connect with some type of higher power. One moment, I am feeling small and insignificant, and the next, I am one with the universe. Everything suddenly falls into place, and I know what I need to do in order to reach Azrael and get home to him.

Sasha smiles. "What do you see?"

"I see Aliyah and Isaiah stepping through the golden light. They have returned to our human realm although Aliyah is no longer human."

"Good. What else do you see?"

"I see Kate sad and isolated behind a wall that keeps her from all of us. She is trapped like me."

Sasha tilts her head to the side as if considering that information carefully.

"I see everything at once, and I know that the secret of our universe is the reality that we are all connected from the smallest ant to the most powerful gods—we are literally one. One consciousness. One universal knowledge."

"Good. Now focus your energy. Is there anything more that the universe is communicating to you?"

I concentrate and then smile. "Within this knowledge, I can see a black gemstone lodged in a wall of crystal amethyst in a cave deep within Deveon. The cave can be reached by a series of waterways and pools. The black gemstone represents my own self love and acceptance." I know without a doubt that I must get this gemstone in order to open the hell dimension and reach Azrael.

"Great work, Nyx. It is a quest. We must accomplish this in order to complete the respect bond and bring your lover to you."

"The gods had said I was back in the game. Somehow I know that, to out play them in a game only they knew the rules to, I will need my mate. We will need to bond and become one, and I will, without question, need to escape this hell dimension."

Sasha smiles and squeezes my hand. I am grateful for her presence. Now all we need to do is ascend to a place of knowledge and power and ultimately transcend, all without the ability to release my Deveon warrior. Ok. Not a problem. Game on, bitches.

Chapter Seventeen

Confrontation

Azrael

"What do you mean they aren't here?" Aliyah asks, panic clear in her voice.

Aliyah and Isaiah had stepped through the trans-dimensional portal and into our living area just a few minutes ago. She looks good. Really good. She wouldn't be back without having released her true Deveon demon, and yet she's still Aliyah. A bigger-than-life version with power and strength emanating from her, and yet still our girl. Interesting. Isaiah is himself again. He is in Deveon form with strength and more power than I've seen him possess in centuries.

"Honestly, we don't know. Nikki and Kate both disappeared weeks ago. They were in the gym and then poof. Az and Nikki had plans to meet up and then nothing. We haven't heard from them since," Rafa tells Aliyah.

"Weeks ago? Good gods, how long have we been gone?" Aliyah asks, surprised.

Isaiah tightens his grip on her hand, and she turns to him. "Time moves differently in different dimensions, babe. It's probably been close to a month since you left the human dimension," he tells her softly.

"Three weeks and two days. Nik and Kate disappeared a week and a half ago. Just *poof*—gone. Nothing missing. No trace of them on the surveillance cams. Nothing." My voice is monotone. I'm just drained. Scared. Lost without her.

Aliyah turns and watches me, her eyes giving away the changes in her the most. They were a soft brown, and now they are glowing gold, her face like porcelain stone. It's hard to get used to.

Isaiah turns to me. "They have to be close by. Do you think it has something to do with the Anhelios? Maybe they sensed our bonds and decided to strike before we had a chance to return?"

Aliyah nods. "We'll find them. Nyx and Keyra must be alive. I can feel them, but it feels distant, wrong. I can feel your bond as well, Azrael. It is strong and pure," Aliyah tells me with a soft smile.

I'm jealous that Aliyah can feel my mate when I haven't been able to reach her. I shake off the strange feelings and smile tightly at my friends. "I think the Anhelos are hiding them. Maybe they realized who Nikki and Kate are and are keeping them contained with some type of magic. I don't know, but I want to go after them." Anger pulses under my skin.

Aliyah watches me. "How many bonds?" she asks simply, and I know without a doubt that Aliyah knows Nikki and I have been secretly bonding. Isaiah looks surprised and glances between the two of us as if I suddenly sprouted multiple heads.

I nod and swallow. "Three. The first was an accident. We didn't even know we could bond when it happened. The second was lust."

The bonds are powerful and hard to resist. Painful even. Aliyah and Isaih are well aware. She nods and I continue, "The third was acceptance, and she must have had an epiphany because it happened while I was at the gym with Rafa ..."

"Yep, apparently we can be bonded without our consent or participation," Rafa says somewhat bitterly, and Aliyah laughs at his obvious discomfort.

"Ah, my dear friend, I can assure you that the bonds do not work like that. Whatever decision Nyx came to without Azrael's presence was something he was in complete agreement with. Am I right, Az?" Aliyah says with a smile.

"Yes. I accepted Nikki a millenia ago. I want us bonded. Nothing was done without work, dedication, and love. I already told this fool that. He is just terrified of the bonds."

Isaiah laughs harshly, but Aliyah looks at Rafa with concern. "You don't want to bond with Keyra?"

"It's not that. Keyra and I never bonded before we became Fallen. We didn't decide to fall in love or choose one another the way the four of you did. She was never my lover. I want to *want* to bond with her, but it feels forced. The Anhelos are threatening an apocalypse. We are sworn to protect humanity. I will have to spend eternity with her." Rafa's voice trails off, and we all stare at him.

"Fuck, man. I didn't know you felt that way," I say as the pieces of his resistance fall into place.

Rafa turns away. "It's all good, man. We'll figure it out. Keyra and I will, when we find them," he says, indicating that his part in this conversation is over.

I nod. "Ok. Welcome home, Aliyah. Isaiah, glad you're back to normal."

Isaiah wraps his arms around Aliyah from behind, fully restored to himself for the first time since Aliyah's rejection months ago.

"But we have work to do. I'm heading to question the Anhelos. Fuck the consequences. You guys coming?" I ask over my shoulder as I head out of the house.

· · · ·

We've been sitting on the Anhelios compound for days, and there have been no sightings of the girls or any unusual movement. I keep reaching out to Nikki telepathically to see if our bond is reopened and nothing. I'm so lost. She is just gone.

"What are you thinking, Az? Are we doing this?" Rafa asks.

"Yeah. I don't want to wait any longer. I don't want those angel pricks hurting them any more than they already have."

"Sun's down, man. Let's give it another 20 minutes, and then we'll have the dark as a cover," Rafa replies from the back of the van where he is monitoring the inside of the Anhelio compound. "You sure they are still, like, alive?" Rafa cringes at the implication that they may not be.

"Honestly, I have no way of knowing. We completed three bonds in this lifetime and when we were still Anhelios. It's just not enough. One more fucking bond, and I'd be linked to her for eternity. I'd know when she dies and when she is reincarnated. I'd know her anywhere. This is fucked up. Somehow it feels wrong though. I don't think she died. At least not in this realm." I'm frustrated at the lack of power I have over all of this.

"What do you mean 'this realm'? Are you thinking they're in a different dimension?"

"I don't know. Maybe. Maybe the Anhelos are hiding them here. There's only one way to find out, right?" I step out of the SUV and slide my sword into the holster on my back, several knives into a thigh holster, and a gun at my back.

"Right," Aliyah responds behind me, and I almost jump out of my skin.

"Gods, woman. Give a guy a little warning," I tell her as I calm my racing heart with deep breaths and smile tightly at Aliyah and Isaiah who joined us just as Rafa and I were exiting the car.

"Toughen up, Demon. We have Deveon warriors to find." She laughs and squeezes my shoulder on the way past.

I snort in response, "Hilarious." Toughen up. Gods, I'm 6'5", 180 pounds of muscle, and thousands of years old.

Aliyah calls back over her shoulder, "Hurry up, lover boy, we've got Anhelo asses to kick." We all rush to catch up to her.

"So, we're not doing this stealthily? We're just barging in?" I ask as we walk up to the compound.

"No point in being discreet. It's time to let these fuckers know I'm back and that there will be consequences for their audacity in taking what's ours. Twice."

We step up to the front entrance of the compound and walk right in.

The Anhelos compound is impressive yet cold. The entrance is all white, white marble floors, and tall beams with huge skylights. The decor is sparse and minimalistic. We move through the front rooms and make our way to the center of the compound. There is a wall of glass doors that open into an indoor swimming area. The flooring is all white marble, and the skylights are open across the entire ceiling of the room, allowing the evening sky to be seen from below. There are four Anhelos spread out around the pool, waiting for our arrival.

"Deveons, you've returned. Did you wish for another beating?" Margot asks cooley from a lounge chair under the pergola. She is blond, her hair plaited in braids on either side of her head. Her features are sharp and exquisite. Her eyes are a dark blue and appear almost black from where I stand across from her. She wears all black—a long, lightweight tunic and wide legged trousers. Her top is belted with a white, leather, corset-style belt, and her shoes are black heels with red bottoms. She wears expensive gold jewelry and looks like a rich trophy wife.

Aliyah smiles tightly. "Margot. How foolish of you to have forgotten you were the ones to run from our last encounter."

Margot's eyes widen slightly, and she smiles at Aliyah as she turns her attention to her. "Ahh, Aliyah. And how are you doing? Still fighting off that pesky bond with Isaiah?" she asks in a snarky tone.

Aliyah smiles. "I believe you have something that belongs to us, Margot. We don't have time for your ridiculous games. Return our friends, and we will leave you peacefully."

"Oh dear, have you lost the little Hunters you've been training?" she says with a shrill laugh.

Light, musical laughter echoes across the open space, and we turn to see Angelica, an exceptionally beautiful woman with bronze skin, black hair, and dark eyes. She is dressed in a red sheath dress that falls to her calves and fits her perfectly. There is a solid gold cuff on her arm and gold heels on her feet. Her lips and nails are painted a deep ruby red.

I watch her as she stands from the table she has been seated at with Lutheran. Angelica unfolds her long body and takes her time smoothing out her deep red silk dress. Her dark skin appears to glow in the moonlight, and her white teeth flash as she smiles at us. "You have such trouble keeping track of your mates, Deveons. I don't believe I would have much confidence in your ability to protect me were I bound to any of you." Angelica gives an exaggerated shudder apparently at the thought of being bound to us.

Aliyah smiles back sweetly. "Honestly, I cannot imagine any being desiring a bond with any of you."

We hear a slight hiss from the corner where Eliana, the tallest of the women, stands motionless.

Eliana has alabaster skin and long red hair. Her eyes are an icy gray, and she is dressed in white silk pants and a dark blue sleeveless top. She is in exceptionally high heels and has perfectly manicured nails. Her makeup is perfect and her skin flawless. Her face is cold, perfect, and vicious. She is without a doubt one of the most beautiful women imaginable, and yet that beauty is almost ugly in its perfection.

"Your choice to bond is pathetic in its sad, little ploy to defeat us. You are all rather pathetic. We do not have your mates or Hunters or whatever the humans are to you. I should remove your filthy demon heads for disgracing our home with your presence," Eliana replies with a calmness that defies the anger in her statement.

"Why should we believe you don't have our friends?" Isaiah asks as he watches the Anhelios from Aliyah's side.

"We don't need to take your humans," Margot replies.

I smile coldly. "You've taken them before. And without knowing their significance to us. Why should we believe you don't have them now?" I am angry and tired of the games.

All three sets of eyes fall on me, and the Anhelios' lips turn up in what should be a smile, but I'm actually not sure anything that friendly would describe their expressions as they look at me.

"We don't care much what you believe, Azrael. Your humans have ruined our little breeding experiment and that is an annoyance," Angelica tells me.

Margot steps forward. "But we do not have them. Perhaps you should track them down before Michael and Gabriel finish healing, I'm sure you will need all the help you can get once we begin our plans," she says with a cold smile

Eliana laughs from where she stands motionless."Which one is your mate, Azrael? I will be sure to hurt her in ways you cannot even imagine, if I find her before you do."

Without thinking, I lunge for her. I have her by the neck and pinned against the wall behind her in the blink of an eye.

"Do not threaten my mate, Eliana. I will not hesitate to remove your head."

Eliana blinks up at me and smiles. Isaiah pulls his sword and holds it at Margot's throat just as Angelica grabs Aliyah.

We all turn as Angelica screams and releases Aliyah, the blue electrical currents still radiating off her skin as she stares at Aliyah in horror. Aliyah laughs as she releases her black and gold wings and smiles at the Anhelios.

"Do not underestimate us, Anhelios. We are more than you can imagine with our pathetic little bonds and love for humanity."

We hear a slow clap from behind us. Lutheran lowers his hands and smiles at us. He is a tall, dark-skinned man with beautiful brown eyes and coarsely braided hair. He wears an expensive mahogany brown suit and crisp white dress shirt

"Well played, Aliyah. Apparently you have awoken and released your demon queen." Lutheran tells her boldly as he steps forward and presses a sword to Isaiah's throat. "But you have overstayed your welcome here. Azrael, please release my friend. Aliyah, I kindly ask you to refrain from touching any members of my family. We do not have your friends. Please leave before I am forced to bleed your mate dry on our very expensive flooring."

Aliyah holds her hands up, and I release the woman standing in front of me

"This isn't over, Eliana. If I find out you are lying about my mate or that you've touched one hair on her head, not even the gods will be able to save you."

She smiles back. "I'll keep my eyes open for Nyx, Azrael. I truly hope I find her first," she tells me with a wink, and it is only the very real threat of the sword to Isaiah's throat that keeps my hands from closing around her throat again.

We follow Lutheran out of the sunroom and through the house in silence until we reach the front entryway and Lutheran releases Isaiah.

"My Queen," Lutheran says as he bows to Aliyah. "It is beyond time we had you back." Aliyah embraces the man we had all considered an enemy just moments ago.

"Lutheran. I am so grateful for your support and sacrifice. Thank you for holding your rank within the Anhelios."

I watch their exchange in shock.

"Yes, my Queen. We do not have much time. The others were telling the truth—we do not have your friends. I would check with the gods themselves. This seems like something they might do to change the outcome of our battle."

"We cannot summon the gods. It would require six original angels, and we do not have the numbers without our friends. You know this Anhelio," I tell him harshly.

"I can be your fifth. Open the bond, Aliyah, and I will meet you at the caves." Lutheran steps back into the doorway and raises his voice. "And stay out you filthy demons, or the next time you will be leaving with considerably less limbs.' he says for what I can only imagine is the

Anhelios' benefit. The door closes in our faces, and Isaiah, Rafa and I all stare at Aliyah in shock.

Chapter Eighteen

The Quest
Nikki

The energy work and grounding had beendraining, and I must have drifted off for a bit. Sasha smiles as I open my eyes.

"Welcome back, Nyx."

"Thanks. So, this is the Challenge? To find the black crystal?"

"It looks like it's all part of the Challenge, Nyx. You have to decide who you can trust," she tells me as she points at herself. "We have to do energy work to access higher knowledge." She waves around to the cave we are in. "And now we have to go on the quest to find the black crystal in the wall of amethyst."

"Ok. So, we follow the labyrinth of water to find the cave with the wall of amethyst. How do we find the water?"

Sasha smiles. "I think we already found it." She gestures to the pool we are seated next to. The cave is large, and the pools of water do seem to be connected.

"Do you have supplies?" I ask hopefully.

Sasha shakes her head. "No, unfortunately. Just what I had on me when I was sentenced. You?"

I shake my head as well. "Just the clothes I was wearing when the gods grabbed me. Thankfully I was in the gym so my running shorts and sports bra will have to do."

"Ok. Let's do this," she says cheerfully, and I smile. Gotta love a go-getter.

. . . . .

The pools and waterfalls are plentiful, and the journey is long. Sasha and I travel for what must be days. This dimension is different from the human's world, and there are layers of earth here. We thought we had lost the path of the waterways at one point until we discovered it was possible to swim down and exit the pools into a similar chamber deeper in the earth.

Everything is something of a riddle that must be unwound in order to see it clearly. It is a bit exhausting.

"Have you traveled to these chambers before?" I ask Sasha, hoping that she is able to guide me.

"No. I was trapped in a different dimension for most of my imprisonment. I was only released when the guys found their way out of Deveon."

I side-eye her and laugh a bit. "Right. You did say that, but that was, what, several hundred years ago, right?"

Sasha laughs freely. "Yes, but time moves differently here. Days here are weeks on earth, sometimes months."

I nod, understanding the gods' motivation on an entirely different level than I had before. "Then this Challenge could simply be the gods' way of distracting Azrael and me while Michael and Gabriel heal?".

"Michael and Gabriel are earth-bound?" Sasha asks with a look of horror on her face.

"Yes. Isaiah beheaded Michael a few months ago, and Rafa stabbed Gabriel through the heart. They have been MIA while healing, but the guys think their time is coming to an end. We expect them to come back with a vengeance soon."

The crisscross of waterways has led us deeper into the caves and chambers, and we must choose which direction to follow. Instinctually I choose the pathway to the left, and Sasha follows.

"They are not wrong. Has there been any contact since they went MIA?" Sasha asks as we make our way over a substantial pile of rock and debris.

"Michael has dream-walked with Aliyah, and I can feel Gabriel's presence. I can't speak to him, but I sense him close."

I actually haven't said this out loud to anyone yet and am surprised by my candor.

Sasha smiles. "Don't be alarmed. I am an empath, after all. Humans have difficulty not sharing with me. I promise I'm safe. You share less than most though, so I am assuming you aren't much of a trusting soul, huh?"

I laugh. "That's putting it mildly. Are you afraid of Michael and Gabriel?"

Sasha shudders. "I'm a Deveons Warrior and an empath so not much frightens me. The Anhelios though are truly evil. It would be wise to keep your distance."

"Not much chance of that though, is there?" I ask with a tight smile. "The apocalypse is coming. The gods are testing us, and it appears that my sole purpose on earth is to bond with my fated mate and release the Deveon goddess warrior, Nyx. Any chance you know if that will kill me?" I ask her with a nonchalance I don't actually feel.

Sasha reaches out and squeezes my shoulder. "It's a lot, I'm sure. You are the Deveons warrior, Nyx. You're not really releasing her so much as stepping into your rightful existence. The gods cheated you, Aliyah, and Keyra. The rest of us have essentially stayed the same. We remember. But when you and Azrael complete the bonds, you will understand. You three are the biggest threat to the gods' plans and to whatever hell the Anhelios have created for humanity. It's why you suffered the greatest sentencing. The bonds though are a gift and a curse."

"You believe we suffered the worst, and yet you have been trapped in hell for centuries?"

Sasha laughs. "This dimension is lonely, but it's not as bad as the humans would have you believe. It's not the same type of loneliness as being stripped of your memories, your powers, and your destiny." Sasha's eyes are wet with tears. And she hugs me tightly, forcing us to stop walking. "You're going to see, Nikki, the world is bigger than you have been led to believe. Once you release your true being, everything truly will fall into place."

I hugged my new friend back. I'm not a hugger, but she seems to bring out a softness I didn't know I possessed. "I hope we can free you from this dimension, Sasha. I hope you can join us in our fight to save humanity. I have a sneaky suspicion that we need you." She steps back and wipes her tears away.

"Oh you absolutely will," Sasha replies with a soft smile that has more sadness than hope. I'm suddenly not sure I want the burden of remembering our past if it gives me the same sadness.

I am about to tell Sasha this when her smile widens and she points to the wall of the cave to our right. "Nikki, look."

I turn to see purple amethyst stones embedded in the wall of the cave. They are scattered and nowhere near the amount I saw in my vision, but they are definitely there.

I smile and step towards the purple stones when Sasha laughs and grabs my hand, dragging me in the direction of them. I laugh and run to keep up with her. We trip through a small doorway and along yet another water path. Finally we reach the end of the waterways and find a small doorway that we have to climb through. The small doorway opens into a huge cave. The walls are covered in purple amethyst, and the floor is a pool of emerald water.

"I don't see the black stone." I tell Sasha, and she turns to smile at me.

"It's here, Nikki. It has to be."

I squeeze her hand before turning my attention back to the stones all around me.

"I honestly don't know where to start."

"I get that. You're a warrior at heart, and this Challenge is more of an inward acceptance and understanding. It's kind of more my field of experience. Which I suppose is why I was drawn to the water caves when you arrived. Maybe this Challenge is more of a gift than we thought. Kind of a crash course in energy work and powers rather than fighting skills."

I process what she is saying and am inclined to agree. I sit by the emerald water and cross my legs, drawing in a long breath and releasing it with a sigh. "Ok. If this Challenge is all about self-reflection and acceptance, then I'm guessing that in order to find the black stone, I need to open my third eye and bring in knowledge," I tell her as I open one eye to observe her reaction.

Sasha laughs and sits down across from me to mimic my stance. "Sounds right to me. Where do you want to start?"

I close my eyes again and focus on my breathing. When my heartbeat slows to match my breaths and I feel a tingling sensation of relaxation flowing through me, I begin to hum. It sounds like a buzzing, and vibrates through my body as I envision the same golden light as before flowing down through the top of the cave and flowing over and around Sasha and me.

I allow the golden energy to flow down through the top of my head and down and around my eyes and cheekbones, flowing back behind my ears and along my jaw. I allow the energy to wash over me and flow through my entire body until I imagine any excess energy flowing down and around my hips and waist and then flowing out of me and returning to the earth beneath me.

"Perfect. Nice energy transference." I open my eyes to smile at her. "Now what's next?" she asks as she guides me.

I close my eyes and focus my energy and thoughts to my third eye, the space between my eyes on my forehead. I imagine a beautiful violet light there, and I push lightness and brightness into the chakra until it bursts with color and light. When this happens, I feel an instantaneous click and know in my heart that I have just completed another bond with Azrael. I open my eyes in surprise, and Sasha smiles.

"That's a really good sign. If I had to guess, Azrael is highly connected to you and is working just as hard as you are at completing his own inner Challenges in order to bring you home. Maybe you just completed the respect bond? What you are doing now without guidance or training would require you to tap into Azrael's power and energy. If you can do that without him here, then your connection is stronger than I thought. Try to use his powers of sight to envision the future."

I blow out a breath and bite the inside of my cheek. "I don't know how he does the casting."

"Well, when I am connected to another being and trying to understand or heal them through the connection, I visualize myself doing exactly that. So if you want to cast out and see your future, then I would envision yourself running your fingers along the amethyst stones until you come to the black stone."

I nod and close my eyes again. I focus on the purple energy in my third eye and envision myself floating up and out of my physical body. I look down and see myself seated on the cave floor with Sasha. I watch us as a golden rope extends from her solar plexus to mine. The golden energy is connecting us, and I wonder if I have a similar connection to all of my Deveon family. I allow myself to move above the water and come to the wall of stones on the other side.

One by one, I envision myself running my hands over the stones. As I get closer, they are almost white—a violet purple on the outside of the stones and a deep purple deeper in the stone. As I work, I imagine Azrael at the compound. I see him smiling at me and coaching me. I see us the first night of our bond when the lust of the bond had us pinned to the wall and touching, tasting, feeling.

A tear slips down my cheek at the possibility that I will never touch him again.

I remember the first night we climaxed together, and I can see us in the water of the pool. I watch in my mind's eye as he pulls me under the waterfall and pushes me against the rock, my body responding to his touch as if it has always belonged to him. I smile as a piece of the puzzle snaps into place, and I realize the importance of water in our connection. The waterfall, the climax.

I open my eyes and look at the cave around me. It's just the pool of water and the wall of amethyst. Shaking my head, I close my eyes again and listen.

I wait.

And then I can hear it. I hear the crash of water against rock coming from a distance, and I smile as I open my eyes. "Let's go." I stand and move towards the back of the cave.

Sasha looks confused. "It's just a wall, Nikki. There's no exit."

I look around. She's not wrong, and yet I can feel the water. I can hear the waterfall. I know that it's the answer to this Challenge.

I look at the clear emerald water and smile. It has to be the answer.

Stripping my clothing off, I leave it at the edge of the water and step into the pool. I walk carefully and navigate the water. I dive down and run my hands along the rock until I find a passageway. It's not very big, and the thought of swimming into an enclosed tunnel terrifies me.

I swim back up and break the surface of the water. "There's another passageway. It's a tunnel, I think. I'm going to swim through and see if it opens on the other side of the cave wall."

Sasha nods and moves to the edge of the water. "I'll come with you."

I shake my head. "There's not enough room. I think I have to do this alone."

"I don't like it, Nik. Maybe there's another way."

"I don't think so. Give me a few minutes to try to clear the tunnel. If I make it through, I'll call back to you."

Sasha nods, and I dive down and make my way through a dark tunnel. The tunnel is long, and as I swim, I can feel the walls of the tunnel all around me. I am starting to get claustrophobic and have been holding my breath for a bit when I start considering using the walls to push myself back through the tunnel and find another way.

Just then, the tunnel appears to have some light at the end, and I force myself to keep going. As I reach the end of the tunnel and push myself up to the surface of the water, I gasp in large gulps of air and look around at the cavern I have emerged in.

Just like I imagined, there is a large waterfall towards the back of the cave, and the light that spills in through the top is beautiful. It flows down into the cave and makes the crystals in the rock walls appear to glow with a lavender haze.

I smile and concentrate my energy on letting Sasha know I am fine. Once I have opened the Deveons bond, I send her an image of the room. She sends back a warm feeling of gratitude.

Smiling, I take in my surroundings and am surprised to see the black crystal stone in the cave wall to my right. It stands out against the purple crystals like a gaping hole in the wall, and I move closer to touch the stone with my fingertips. I am considering how to wedge the stone free when I am hit with an onslaught of memories that make my knees weak.

As I am processing the multitude of memories, I am hit with a particularly male, violent one. As I steady myself in this cavern alone in Deveon, I see myself before the War of the Winged Beasts. It feels like the same time period as the memories I shared with Azrael. Sometime around our original bonding a millenia ago.

I am walking along a shore with Gabriel. We are barefoot and strolling along the edge of the water. I laugh as the water kisses my ankles and calves. Gabriel smailes at my antics. Our friendship seems comfortable, as if we have known one another a long time and share good times. He laughs and pulls me closer to him on the shore so that the waves do not come up as high on my legs.

"Nyx, be serious for a moment. I want to talk to you about the future."

I stare at him in confusion. "What type of future Gabe?"

"We have been friends for as long as I can remember, and you have always been a worthy opponent and good Anhelio. You have followed the directions of the gods without all this nonsense of Aliyah and her traitors. It is time I shared with you the plans of our people." His tone is more serious than I have heard it in the past.

I stare at him and swallow hard. "What type of plans, Gabriel?" I ask again, and he smiles. I have never thought much about our ways or my friend's expressions, but the look he gives me now causes shivers to run along my spine.

He grasps my hand and continues to walk. I follow along. "We have chosen to deny the humans their humanity so to speak. Aliyah and her traitors have done the unthinkable and given the humans the gift of knowledge. They now believe they are something more than our servants and slaves. It is ridiculous, really, but if the traitors want to start a war over these livestock, then so be it."

I swallow down a sense of dread and repulsion at his words. "What are you planning to do, Gabe?" My voice is louder than I intend.

Gabriel laughs and smiles at me. "We have decided that since humans now have knowledge of their own sexuality and can be bred, we will breed them. We will create a new race of archangels who are superior to humans in every way. Essentially removing humans from the equation entirely," he tells me with pride.

I choke back my disgust and drop my friend's hand.

"How can this be true? What is wrong with you? The gods will never allow you to do this. It is wrong. They are people who deserve to exist as much as we do." I am shocked at his words.

Gabriel sneers at me. "You are a fool. Of course the gods will approve our plan, and if they do not, then let them strike us down," he tells me arrogantly as he spins in a circle and swings his arms wide to the heavens.

"Gabriel, this is anarchy. We were never intended to destroy humans. They have evolved and are becoming important outside of our needs. Why not release them from their chains? Why can't we simply let them go?" I ask him desperately, attempting to help him see reason.

"No. The gods can not deny a sacrifice, and we will sacrifice the humans to make them a more intelligent, more loyal race of beings."

"What do you mean they cannot deny a sacrifice?"

Gabriel shakes his head at my perceived ignorance. "If an Anhelio, or perhaps even a human," he says with disgust, "makes a sacrifice to the gods that is greater than their perceived worth, then the gods must accept it. It is simply the way of the gods."

I watched him skeptically. "How do you know this?"

Gabriel throws his head back and laughs. "We have been busy preparing for war, Nyx. I thought that you were one of us. That you could be trusted. Can you not?" he asks with a look of disgust.

I shake my head at this man whom I had considered a friend for as long as I can remember. "No. Gabriel, I will not help you with a genocide. I will not be an accomplice to the horrors you describe."

Before I can do much of anything, Gabriel pulls his sword, and I jump back as it nicks my throat. I remove two knives from a holster on my thigh and expertly spear him just above the heart.

"Think twice, friend, before you attempt to threaten a warrior," I tell him, and he sneers at me.

"You are nothing more than one of Aliyah's loyal dogs. I had so many hopes for you, Nyx. I had hoped you would help us breed this new species, and now I find you are nothing more than a traitor."

"I will gladly take the title of a dog to Aliyah's cause if this is the alternative you and the others have agreed upon. This is disgusting and wrong. I will not aid you in this forsaken path." I aim the other knife at his heart. "We are through, Gabriel. You are not the being I believed you to be, and I am clearly not what you thought of me."

He backs away slowly, vibrant red blood trickling around the knife in his chest. "You will come to regret this, Nyx."

The memory fades away to reveal another. In this memory, I am suited in leather armor and am violently cutting down the humans, archangels, and Anhelios that oppose the vision Aliyah has for humanity. Sasha fights at my side, and the scars, blood, and damage are profound.

We are covered in our enemies' blood and have been fighting for several days and nights when Gabriel suddenly appears before us. Sasha steps forward to shield me from this madman who has been after me since our friendship dissolved on that beach months ago.

Gabriel throws his head back and laughs at my friend and fellow warrior. "This imbecile is who you trust to protect you, Nyx? I would have chosen a better guard, old friend," he tells me with a gleam in his eye. Something in his tone has me afraid.

"Show some respect. Sasha has fought fearlessly beside me for the entirety of the war, and I trust her with my life." I spit out at Gabriel before he reaches for his sword and impales my friend through the chest.

Sasha lets out a cry that can only be called a wail as the air seeps from her lungs, and she crumbles to the ground at my feet. My own sword is in my hand, and I lunge at the madman before me.

He laughs giddily. "Sacrifice." He squeals, the sound of a lunatic as he spreads his huge wings and soars away from us. I am surprised—I had expected him to come for me once my friend was incapacitated. Turning, I find Aliyah and Azrael at my back and now understand his departure. I am an impressive warrior, but Gabriel is insane with an ax to grind.

Tears splash down my face at my friend's limp and twisted body. "Sasha has been a true friend and warrior. She was a compassionate and powerful empath with powers beyond my comprehension."

Aliyah squeezes my arm. "We all knew the consequences when we decided to fight for humanity, Nyx. Sasha made her choice. Her sacrifice will never be forgotten."

The image fades, and I sink to my knees to the cavern floor in pain. The hard stone presses against my skin, and the rough sting is enough to remind me I am in a hell dimension, fighting to find a way out or trying to bring my lover to me.

I hear laughter behind me, and I turn my head sadly to see Gabriel standing ten feet away, smirking at me.

"Is it all too much, Nikki? Was the onslaught of memories and emotions too much for your sensitive humanity?" He taunts me from his place across the pool.

"Fuck off, Gabe. I wish I had known all this when we were in the dungeon. I would have killed you if given half a chance." The rawness of my anger is choking me.

Gabriel laughs. "Oh, you and me both, Nyx. Had I known who you were when I had you chained to a wall and under my command, I would have had so much more fun with you." He smirks at me, sucking on his teeth.

I suppress the shiver that makes its way along my spine and rise from the ground. I glare at the being across from me. "How are you here, Gabe? I was sure Rafa put a knife through your heart months ago." I taunthim with the memory.

Gabriel smirks and shrugs his shoulders. "Maybe your boy didn't do the level of damage you assumed. Maybe I'm here to finally finish you off before the gods' Challenge restores your powers." He smiles a slow, dangerous smile, "Maybe I've decided to make you the sacrifice to the gods you were always meant to be." His words are intended to put fear in my heart, and they do. They are also incredibly telling.

I smile my own slow smirk at the madman sharing this deserted cave with me and step closer to him. "I'd bet my left tit that you aren't actually here. If you were, Gabriel, then I would assume you would be doing more damage than simply slinging insults and jabs." I reach for him, and he mimes grabbing my hand. I side step, and he laughs.

"You sure about that, sweetheart?"

"Pretty fucking sure. So that means you must be dream-walking which means my powers are increasing. I'm getting stronger. Azrael and I are bonding without even touching or being in the same fucking realm. Is that scaring you, Gabe? Are you so terrified of our combined power that you had to use your own energy, which you could be using to heal, to come here and what, taunt me?" The emotions combine to overwhelm me.

Gabe sucks at his teeth and smirks again. "Careful, Nyx. I'm watching, and very soon I won't have to dream-walk in order to get to you. I'll be able to waltz on over to your Deveon compound and slit your pretty little throat while your lover sleeps next to you."

I smile back. "You'd better hurry, bitch. I'm incredibly close to my last bond, and then slitting my throat would only delay me in making my sole purpose in life your daily torment," I tell him with way more moxie than I actually have.

Gabriel tisks at me, "Now, now, Nyx. No need for threats. I just wanted to drop by and remind you that sacrifice is important to the gods. Maybe yours, maybe someone you love. Either way I win, old friend, I just wanted you to hear it from me."

With that, Gabriel is gone. He simply vanishes, and the relief I feel is overwhelming. I sink to my knees again, and using the last of my energy, I call out to Azrael before the blackness closes in and I sink into the velvety arms of unconsciousness.

I know I'm vulnerable. I know that naked and exposed in a cave somewhere in Deveon isn't the safest place to welcome a respite from my current state of affairs. I just don't have the mental or emotional capacity to process all this without allowing the darkness in. I can only hope that having completed my quest and discovering the black stone will be enough to keep me safe as I slowly slip away, hoping that the powers that be will protect me from all the things that go bump in the night. I'm just starting to realize, I may very well be one of those things.

Chapter Nineteen

The Summons

Azrael

"Nikki has been gone for almost a month, and I haven't felt her existence through the bond at all. How is this possible?" I ask Aliyah as I pace the kitchen while Aliyah is making coffee.

"I don't know, Az. If she were here, in this realm, then we should both be able to feel her through the Deveon bonds. Perhaps she is in a different realm or dimension. If so, time moves differently in different realms. My third bond allowed Isaiah and me to communicate telepathically. Were you able to talk to her?" Aliyah asks thoughtfully.

"Yes. From our first bonding I could hear and feel her, but it wasn't until the third bond that she could hear me. That was just before she disappeared." The anxiety increases with my pacing.

Aliyah reaches out and grips my forearm. I stop pacing, and she smiles at me. "Azrael, we are doing everything we can to find her and Kate. If the Anhelios don't have her—and I believe Lutheran that they do not—then it must be the work of the gods. We are working on a summons, but it is difficult. Lutheran has agreed to be our fifth, but we need six willing Anhelios or Deveons to summon the gods. This measure was put in place to make summoning them to deal with petty disputes nearly impossible. Unfortunately, the gods' idea of a petty dispute and ours are very different."

"Can you open the bond and call Lutheran?"

"Already done, friend," Lutheran announces as he walks into the kitchen, followed closely by Rafa and Isaiah. Lutheran smirks, and Isaiah stops him before he gets too close to Aliyah. Isaiah moves in front of Lutheran and pulls a chair from the dining set, indicating he should be seated.

Lutheran smiles at Isaiah. "I do understand your hesitation, Isaiah. But we were once all friends. Can you not remember me as such?"

"Honestly Lutheran, I sincerely appreciate your sacrifice. Were you truly with us all of these years and simply awaiting Aliyah's awakening to return to us, then I applaud your determination and acting skills. Still, you must forgive me for having my doubts," Isaiah tells him.

Aliyah releases my arm and moves past me to her lover and mate. She confidently places a hand on his chest as she moves towards Lutheran. "I, however, do not doubt your genuine and impressive sacrifice my friend." Aliyah allows her hand to fall down Isaiah's arm and to his hand. She squeezes his hand reassuringly. "I am beyond grateful to you for keeping your rank within the Anhelios and allowing us to have an inside man throughout all of this."

Lutheran bows his head in acknowledgement "There is much to talk about. The Anhelios have many knives in the fire and are planning to destroy the human race as soon as Michael and Gabriel return."

Aliyah nods. "Understood, friend. But first we must retrieve our friends. If the gods are playing with us and have taken Nyx and Keyra, then we must get them back before anything can be done to stop the Anhelios plans."

I clear my throat from my place in the kitchen and nod towards Lutheran. "I appreciate your difficult situation, man, although I'm not sure I can untangle the years of war, destruction, and bullshit you have been a part of since the War of the Winged Beasts. My priority is finding Nyx and Kate. How can you help us when we need six to open a summons?"

Lutheran levels me with his gold eyes. "If Nyx and Kate are your priority, friend, which of them is your mate?".

I frown at his questioning. "I'm not sure what difference it makes to you. Why would we give you more information that you can take back to the Anhelios?"

Lutheran snorts out a laugh. "I have no desire to take anything back to the Anhelios. I do, however, have a vested interest in Keyra and her safety. We were once lovers, and she was my motivation to join your revolution." Lutheran turns to Aliyah. "I am, of course, loyal to your cause, my Queen. I will help you find them even if my woman has chosen Azrael or Rafa as her mate. I do, however, need to know that before the summons. My priorities are true."

I can feel the tension release from my back and neck at his confession. If he and Keyra were lovers, then it makes sense that he would return to us with Aliyah's awakening and Kate's disappearance.

I turn to look at Rafa and am surprised by the tension he holds at the announcement. I had thought he felt nothing for Keyra and was opposed to their bonding. This should be a relief to him, and yet he looks uncomfortable with the current turn of events.

I return my attention to Lutheran. He looks uncomfortable with my silence, and his eyes have turned a bit colder. I smile tightly. "Nyx is my lover and fated mate. I am concerned for both of them though, and it is my intention to bring them both back once we can locate them."

Lutheran nods and reaches into his pocket to bring out a vial of blood. "This is Margot's blood. I believe it may be possible to summon the gods with a loophole.".

Aliyah nods. "It might work."

Suddenly there is a flash of light, and a portal opens in the kitchen. We turn as one to watch as a woman stumbles through the portal and looks around confused. "Aliyah?" she asks as she steps into the kitchen, and the portal closes behind her. We stare at her in shock.

"Sasha? How is this possible? You were killed before the War of The Winged Beasts. I watched Gabriel do it myself," Aliyah responds in shock.

Sasha looks around at the five of us in utter confusion. "I honestly have no idea. I know you all. I feel love and kinship towards you. I can recall your names, and yet I have no idea how I know you. I'm reaching for a memory to connect to you, but it's just out of reach."

Rafa steps forward to catch her as she stumbles. I could swear an electrical current flows between them, but when I blink, any trace of it is gone.

"Wow, darling," Rafa exclaims as Sasha collapses. He swoops her up and carries her to the couches in the living area. Sitting with her as she acclimates, Rafa pulls a chenille throw blanket from the back of the couch to cover her when he notices she's trembling. "What the hell happened to you, darling?"

She sighs. "I honestly have no idea. My memories are gone. I don't know what I was doing or where I was before I walked through the portal, and I don't have any recollection from my life before that." Her eyes fill with tears, and she blinks them away. "What is the War of the Winged Beasts?"

I sigh and turn to the stove to make some tea. I can tell this is going to be a very long day.

"On the bright side, if she is in Anhelios form and not a human, then we can use her as the sixth in our summoning of the gods," a voice says from behind me, and I nod to Lutheran without looking.

"Yes. If she is still one of us, we can ask her to help summon the gods. We don't actually use women without their consent though," I tell him, still angry at the centuries of betrayal.

Lutheran nods, "Of course, Azrael. I misspoke."

"Gods, so you have been one of us for centuries, and you lived and worked with the Anhelios as if nothing happened?"

"Yes. They are bat-shit crazy. I'm fairly certain that they know I hold that opinion, but as long as I do not get in the way of their plans, they tolerate me."

"Fuck. That's dedication, man." I open the canister holding the tea leaves and fill the tea ball before adding it to the hand-painted earthenware mugs.

Lutheran watches me. "You were in Deveon. Aliyah, Nyx, and Keyra were humans, destined to be reborn for centuries until Isaiah and Aliyah could bond. Or so we all believed until you and Nyx began accumulating powers while Aliyah and Isaiah were gone." Lutheran stops and swallows hard. "It hurts to know Kate was in our compound being mistreated right under my nose and we could have been something different."

I turn to stare at him, "Lutheran, you are not Fallen. Had you known Kate was Keyra and had the two of you bonded, the Anhelios would have gained power, not us. You realize this, right? If you are truly one of us, then we have to find a way to make you a Deveon before you and Keyra bond or the powers will go to the wrong side."

"I understand. Keyra may not choose me as her mate, friend. I was simply saying, knowing we could have been closer, that I could have protected her. It would have made the isolation and loneliness less disheartening."

I sigh. "I am so sorry for your situation. I can't imagine being with the Anhelios and suffering their unjust and disgusting ways for centuries as a means to keep a promise to our queen. It couldn't have been easy." I hand him a mug of tea.

"Thank you, Azrael. I will do everything in my power to help bring your mate and my woman back to us."

I choose not to mention we had believed, until his confession, that Rafa and Keyra were fated mates. Time would tell how that particular situation would play out. For now, we needed him to summon the gods. I turn away and carry several mugs into the living area for Sasha and Raf.

"So you do know magic and energy work, but you don't remember anything else?" Aliyah asks Sasha.

"I *know* that I know how to transfer energy, ground and cleanse the chakras, and move through dimensions. I just don't know how I know this. I have no memories to base it on," Sasha says with a shrug.

Aliyah smiles encouragingly. "Do you know if you are Anhelio, Deveon, or something else?"

"What else could she be?" I ask as I hand Sasha a mug of tea. "She can't be human or she wouldn't have been able to trans-dimensional teleport. If she survived the War of the Winged Beasts, then she must be Deveon. The gods cursed all the angels and archangels who fought with us as Fallen. Sasha fought with us until just moments before the gods themselves intervened."

Aliyah nods. "But I traveled to Deveon while still human," she points out.

"True. But you were unable to return to the human realm without releasing your true Deveon form. If that was true for Sasha, if she were human, she couldn't have come here to the human dimension without releasing her true Deveon form."

We all turn to look at Sasha expectantly. "How do I do that?" she asks. "Release my Deveon form?"

Aliyah smiles. "Concentrate on your inner power. See it as a lightness and brightness in your chest, and then see that energy as a ball of light." Aliyah walks Sasha through a process I wouldn't know how to articulate even after having done it for millenia. Perhaps being 'new', allowed her to see the process differently.

"Good. Now allow the light to take on a color based on the type of power you are calling forth—purple for knowledge, green for empathy, red for more base emotions like fear, anger or frustration. Good. Focus on the color now and push it outward." Aliyah demonstrates by pushing her arms out in front of her.

I raise an eyebrow and smirk, but Isaiah gives a mental shake of his head. Sasha sits forward, the blanket falling to the ground as she pushes outward with her mind's eye. I feel the slap of her power and involuntarily take a step back as her wings spring forth and beautiful, twisted, black bone horns emerge from her porcelain forehead. The black bone is a sharp contrast to her fair complexion, fiery red hair, and green eyes. Her black and gold wings are breathtaking, and we all smile at our long lost friend.

"Apparently she's Deveon. So the gods damned her to where, Deveon?" I ask, bewildered by this turn of events.

"She couldn't have been. We would have known, and she wasn't there while we were imprisoned," Isaiah says in confusion.

"Well, wherever she's been, she's here now, and we are grateful," Aliyah says softly.

Sasha smiles, and Rafa reaches out, his fingers barely brushing a wing feather before he snatches his hand back. "May I?" he asks, and Sasha nods as he gently strokes her wings. "So damn beautiful," he murmurs.

"Will you help us, Sasha? My fated mate Nyx, and her friend Keyra, have disappeared, and we must summon the gods to find them."

"Yes, but I don't know how I can help though."

"We need six original angels to summon the gods. There are four of us Deveons, and Lutheran, an Anhelio, makes five. If you would go with us to the caves to summon the gods, we would have six," I say.

"I think I can do that. Are the gods kind?"

Lutheran snorts. "Sure, if you consider damning the lot of us to hell over attempting to save humanity, which they created, kind."

Sasha looks at him skeptically. "I really don't."

"Even so," Aliyah interrupts, "they are fair, and as long as we are respectful and abide by the rules, they cannot hurt us. They are their rules after all."

I watch them skeptically. Sure, they can't physically hurt us, but they did damn us all to a form of hell. They stole Sashas memories and took Nyx and Keyra when we needed them the most. I am beginning to doubt that the gods are impartial to our vow to save humanity. In fact, I'm beginning to believe that they are actively working to prevent our success. Game on. They have underestimated the Deveons once again. Perhaps we can use that to our advantage.

. . . .

The caves are dark and slightly damp this time of year. I have always loved spring. New energy. New beginnings. Growth. Rebirth. I'm all in.

Still, the caves being what they are, we carry torches to the back of the original caves deep in the desert of Arizona. We place the torches to the dried hay we brought and add a log to the fireplace. The glow of warmth is beautiful. The six of us spread out and display our elements—earth, fire, water, and air—in a circle about ten square feet around. As we pour the water into an earthenware pot, add it to the fire to boil, and cast a swirling magical energy for the air element, we chant and summon the gods. When we have finished, we take turns cutting our hands and spilling our blood onto the fire. And then we wait in silence for the gods to appear.

It doesn't take long.

"How dare you assume to summon us, you ungrateful Demons," Enhil complains as she appears in a white flowing dress, belted at the waist. Her dark hair flows freely down her back.

"Now, now, dear sister, perhaps the filthy demons have something of importance to discuss," Enki says as he materializes next to his sister god. "It has been a millenia, give or take. And they have been successfully moving through the obstacles we set in place, albeit rather slowly." He smirks.

"I don't care what they want. Nothing they have to say carries any importance, and I find them all rather boring," Ishtar announces unsurprisingly.

I shake my head as I step forward. "We did not wish to disturb you, and yet we hope that you can enlighten us as to the location of our human Hunters, Nikki and Kate." I keep my head up, indifferent to their status of gods.

Ishtar laughs, a shrill sound that echoes off the walls of the cave. "Oh, how fun." She claps her hands ``Perhaps I spoke too soon!" she says gleefully.

Enhil nods to her sister, yet addresses me. "And somehow you think that we, as gods, would be bothered to interfere with your little Hunters?" Her words and tone indicate that they are above such trivial matters.

Aliyah steps forward to stand next to me. "Honestly, yes. We do. We should be able to locate their presence through the bonds, and yet the human Hunters are simply gone. The Anhelios claim to have no knowledge of their location. You would be the next reasonable explanation. Have you any knowledge of their whereabouts?" Aliyah asks carefully, using her words to trap the gods into a direct answer.

Enki sighs. "The Hunters have been given the opportunity to advance in this little game of ours. We grew bored with your lack of, shall we say, advancement, and chose to move the game forward."

I clench my fists at my sides. Aliyah squeezes my forearm and smiles at the gods. "So you gave them an opportunity to advance ... what does that mean exactly?"

I simmer with anger and resentment that the gods did, in fact ,steal my mate and our friend to selfishly change the outcome of their *game.*

Ishtar giggles. "Nyx is in a realm of danger and fear. She must overcome her own inner demons, grow as an individual, and complete a quest all as her Challenge to become the Deveon warrior she once was!" she says empathically, her mood improving with her excitement. I watch her, the realization that the gods have become more unhinged over the centuries more and more evident.

"So this realm of danger and fear explains why we can no longer reach her. Is Kate with her?" Aliyah asks carefully.

Enki watches me with amusement. My anger is not lost on the male god.

Enhil shakes her head slightly. "No. The human Hunters must complete their own trials before we can allow them to return to you." she replies almost as carefully as Aliyah.

I grit my teeth with the realization that the gods have no intention of telling us where Nyx and Keyra are.

Aliyah chooses her words carefully, and I am grateful for her presence as I am far too emotional to trust myself to get any real information from the gods. "Is Nikki able to return to the human realm without assistance?"

Enhil hisses and shakes her head. "Very clever, demon Queen. No. Nikki must embrace her Deveon form in order to return to the human realm."

Aliyah nods. "I see. So she is in Deveon. That is the only realm that allows humans and Deveons to pass freely."

"Very good, demon. And yet there are hundreds of realities, or realms, of Deveon, and your time is running out. Tik Tok, Tik Tok." Enki says with a tone of boredom that the excitement in his eyes betrays.

"And Kate, where have you hidden her?" Lutheran asks boldly from his place among us.

Enhil smiles, exposing her sharp pointed teeth. "Ahhh, Lutheran. Why are you here, child? I was under the impression that you had chosen to side with the Anhelios. Were we wrong about that? Are you a fallen angel after all?" She chides him.

Lutheran ignores her and asks again, "Where have you hidden Kate? Is she in a Deveon realm as well?"

Ishtar's laughter rings out, and we all turn to her. "Keyra, in human form, is right in front of your face, you fools. She is here and yet not. She is next to you, silly child. Can you not see her?" She laughs harder, and the other gods ignore her.

"Riddle me this," Sasha says, and all eyes turn to her. The gods laugh at her presence. "How can someone be somewhere and nowhere all at once? Have you lost your mind?"

Enhil hisses at her disrespect, and Rafa moves to stand in front of her as if to protect her from the gods' wrath. "Insolent child. You are the one who has the answers to our riddles, you difficult little empath." She spits insults at Sasha. "You were with Nyx. Her trials are what set you free. You can see your sister Keyra if only you could unlock the secrets hiding in your own mind. Careful what you wish for, child. The truth may be more than any of you are truly ready for," she says as the gods shimmer in and out of corporal form. Our time with them is running out.

"How do we find them?" I ask as the gods fade.

"If Nyx is trying to get back to you, she will find a way to let you know. If not, then nothing we could tell you would help. Tik Tok, Azrael. Humans cannot survive in Deveon for long," Enki replies just as the gods fade from our presence.

I groan in frustration as the gods dissipate, and we are left alone in the caves without much more information than when we came.

"Try to remain calm, Az," Aliyah says as she turns to me. Isaiah steps behind her and wraps his arms around her waist, holding her tightly. "They did tell us that Sasha is the key to finding Nyx and Kate. We just have to help her remember." Aliyah's voice drifts off at the realization that that could take months, and if what the gods said was true about running out of time, then we had perhaps days at best.

"They also said if Nyx was working on finding you, she would. What does that mean to you?" Lutheran asks.

I turn to face the Anhelio just as our fourth bond clicks into place, and I breathe a sigh of relief. A smile spreads across my face as I feel her again for the first time in over a month.

"Thank, gods." I breathe as her memories start coming fast. They are hard truths and many of them painful. I can feel her anguish and despair as they hit her hard. The bond is open again, and I can feel the cave she is in. It is hot, beautiful with the amethyst wall behind her and the black stone of respect and acknowledgement clear in her vision.

I nod to the others, "Deveon, the amethyst caves." I conjure a portal from the energy around us.

"Wait, Azrael. The timing is suspicious. Please wait while we sort this out," Aliyah pleads as I step through the portal into Deveon. Her fears fall on deaf ears.

If only I had more patience. If only I had thought before I moved forward. We'll never know if talking it out would have changed the outcome because it wasn't even an option for me at the time. Hindsight really is 20/20.

Chapter Twenty

Lovers

Nikki

The memories and dream-walking really drained me, and I must have passed out on the floor of the amethyst cave. When I come to, Azrael is holding me.

"Hi," he says softly, and I tear up.

"Are you really here?" I ask him.

He smiles and runs his hands gently through my hair. "I'm really here, babe. Gods, I've missed you so damn much."

I laugh gently. "It's only been a few days, though, right?" I sit up and throw my arms around him.

"No baby, it's been over a month in the human realm. Time moves differently here. Are you ok?" He holds me away from him and searches my face and body for cuts, bruises, anything out of place.

"I'm fine. I am so glad you came though. The gods grabbed me when Kate and I were in the gym. Is she ok?" I ask, worried for my friend.

Azrael shakes his head slightly. "We don't know. A lot has happened since you were taken. Kate disappeared at the same time. We couldn't find either of you. We went to the Anhelios, but they didn't have you."

I cover my mouth with my hand. "Oh no, did anyone get hurt?" I ask, worried for my people.

Azrael smiles and kisses me softly. "No, baby. Everyone is fine. Aliyah and Isaiah ..."

"They're back?" I ask excitedly, and he smiles at me. I grin wider.

"Yes, they're back and better than ever. Aliyah is the Deveon Queen now and has her full powers."

"She has, like, wings and horns and shit?" I interrupt him again, and he laughs.

"Yep. Full demon now," he tells me with a smile.

"And she's still her? Not some strange Deveon entity that's taken over Aliyah's body?" I ask seriously.

Azrael pulls me closer and strokes my hair. "She's still her, baby. Which reminds me. I did feel the last two bonds click into place which brings us to the fifth. I'm not sure if you know where you are exactly, but ..." His voice trails off, and I pull back to look at him

"The gods said that this is Deveon. Which, to be honest, is a bit obvious. Fire and brimstone? Check. Lava? Check. Purple skies and darkness? Check. I haven't seen any demons though." I tease.

Azrael laughs. "Well that's not exactly true, now is it?" He allows his Deveon wings to spring forth and the black horns to protrude from his forehead.

He really is incredibly sexy.

Azrael strokes me with his soft wings, touching my hips, my breasts, the softness of my belly, and I shiver for the first time since being in this ridiculously hot realm. He laughs again and carefully begins to remove his clothing. I bite my lip as he removes his shirt and steps closer to run my fingertips along the planes of his chest. I poke my tongue out to wet my lips, and Azrael growls deep in his chest.

"I need to taste you, babe," he says simply as he sinks his long fingers into my hair and drags my face closer to his. He brushes his lips over mine, more gently than I had expected. He continues to run his lips over mine again and again and then more firmly until I open my mouth to his tongue.

He licks into my mouth, increasing the pressure, and I groan as my need for him builds. I can feel my thighs getting slick with desire as he continues to lick into my mouth, his hands stroking over my body, gently, patiently, much too slowly. I groan again as I reach for his pants and quickly undo the button and the zip. He isn't wearing anything under his pants, and I reach inside to stroke my fingers over his impressive length.

I close my hand around the girth of him, barely able to close my fingers around him. His skin is hot and velvety soft, and I rub my thighs together to try to relieve some of the tension. I can feel his laughter rumble in his chest, and I smile against his lips.

"I want all of this inside me, Az. Gods, I want it. I'm not sure I can take all of you though, babe. This is a lot of cock. I'm not going to lie, I'm a little intimidated."

He releases my mouth and teases his tongue around my tight nipple. He bites gently, and I jump at the sensation.

"You're going to take all of it into your tight, little cunt, Nyx. I'm going to work it in slowly, so fucking slowly. I'm going to make you beg for it. I'm going to work you over so throughly before I let you have it all, and then I'm going to fuck you with this huge cock just the way you like it, baby."

I swear I almost cum at his words alone. Azrael laughs as he flicks my nipple with his forked tongue and sucks at my breast.

"Fuck, Az, that feels amazing."

"I am about to show you truly amazing, Nik."

I wrap a leg around his hip and rub my pussy against his thigh shamelessly. I can feel his soft wings stroking my ass and the back of my thighs, and I swallow back another groan as I drop to my knees and grip his cock in my hand. I open my lips and lick the length of him.

Azrael groans as I tease the head of his cock with my tongue. His hands sink into my hair again, and he nudges me closer as he strokes his thumb along my jaw.

"Do you want to suck my cock, Nikki?"

I nod as I look up at him.

"Open wider, darling. I'm going to slide all the way down that pretty little throat."

My pussy clenches at the promise.

I oblige and open my mouth as wide as I can and wait as he slides his cock past my lips to rest at the back of my throat. I swallow hard and close my lips around him. Azrael groans at the sensation. I smile around his cock and then begin working him over with my lips and tongue. I move up and down the length of him, corkscrewing his cock in and out of my mouth as I lick and suck in time with my movements. I'm getting wetter and more desperate as I work over his cock, bringing him in deeper and deeper until he is halfway down my throat. I swallow back the panic and breathe through my nose.

Azrael stays as still as possible, and I find it amusing as I listen to his shallow breaths and desperate groans. I know he is holding himself back from fucking into my throat, and I'm grateful for the moment. I know it won't be long before I'm begging him to come down my throat, desperate for the taste of him.

"Good gods, woman, you know I can hear your thoughts, right? Keep that shit up and I'll be coating your throat and not that soaking wet pussy with my cum." H

I groan around his cock when I feel his hands sink into my hair and pull me off of his length.

"Enough, baby. I want to taste that pussy."

I stand, and he slips his arms under my thighs and lifts me to his shoulders.

"Ride my face, Nik." His impressive wings slip behind my body and cushion my back and head against the wall of the cave.

I lean back into the cradle of his wings as he smirks at me and then licks my pussy with his forked tongue. Over and over. He laps at me, licking my clit and my pussy until I come apart, screaming his name. The sound echoes off the cave walls, and he smiles at me with a satisfied smirk.

I come down slowly from the height of my climax, and Azrael gently lowers me to the ground, holding me with his arms and wings.

"Good job, baby. I love hearing my name in acapella," he tells me with a genuine smirk.

I laugh. "You think that was impressive? Wait till you get that cock inside me. I have no doubt I'll be hitting all the high notes."

"Good gods, woman, you're fucking killing me." He groans as my legs drop open shamelessly, and my back arches off of the cave floor. I watch him as he carefully slides his thumb along my clit and slips two fingers inside of me. I take his mouth and kiss him while he works me with his fingers.

I'm desperate for him, nudging him with my thighs, trying to get his cock in position as I become more and more desperate. Azrael places his huge hand against my throat, and I swallow hard. Closing my eyes for a moment, I still my movements as he slides his length against me, over and over, his hand tightening on my throat as he slips the tip of his impressive cock inside of me.

"Oh fuck, yes, please," I say without thought.

Azrael chuckles. "Gonna need you to work that tight cunt onto my cock, baby. Ride me like you mean it. I want this on your terms."

Something inside me breaks wide open. I'm not sure how this is something that makes me emotional, but somehow it is like the sweetest expression of love.

I climb to my knees and straddle this demon like it's a damn mission. I slowly lower my hips until the head of his cock breaches me, and then I push down.

"Fuck. That's tight." Azrael breaths out.

I laugh as I move my hips back and forth and up and down, coating his cock so that more of it fits inside me. I can feel myself stretching to accommodate his huge cock, and I groan.

"I want to ride, baby." He laughs and holds my hips for a few moments.

"Give it a minute. I don't know how long I can hold back if you're fucking me with that greedy, little pussy. I want you to feel good, baby. I definitely don't want to hurt you."

"Ok, I'm good," I tell him a few moments later as my pussy clenches around his cock, desperate for more.

Azrael laughs and let's go of my hips so I can fuck myself with that cock. His hand slides to the base of my throat, and he winks. My pussy flutters in anticipation, and then he's lifting his hips and pushing into me in the best way. My body cries out for release, and I come on his cock while he fucks me to his own release.

I smile down at Azrael as I lay sprawled out over his body. "That was amazing."

"I'm genuinely pleased that you think so because that is going to be happening daily for the rest of eternity soooo ..." He winks.

I laugh with him. "Ok, but I think I'm going to be a little sore for the rest of eternity then. Totally worth it, don't get me wrong."

He wraps his arms around me and rolls me until he hovers above me, his wings cushioning my body from the cave floor.

"I love you, Nikki. I do, and I know it might feel like it's too soon for you. I understand that. I just wanted you to know that you are loved. And I promise to cherish you and protect you. You are mine, and I am yours. For eternity," Azrael tells me with the softest tone. He kisses me gently, and my heart cracks wide open.

I choke on my own air and laugh as tears cloud my eyes "I love you too, Az. So damn much." I can feel the fifth bond click into place, and I laugh out loud. "Thank the gods. Just one more and we can join the others at home."

"What if I want you all to myself for just a while longer?" I can feel the hold he has on my heart getting tighter.

I smile back at him. "I think that sounds amazing."

We lay together in silence for a while, and then Azrael squeezes me tightly and takes his feet with me still in his arms.

"I think we should find our clothes and come up with a game plan. We need to complete the last bond in order to get you home."

"I left my clothes in the cave on the other side of ... shit!" I cover my mouth as my eyes go wide. "I left my clothes in the other cave with Sasha. I left Sasha alone for hours." I feel incredibly guilty for forgetting about my new friend.

Azrael laughs at my expression. "It's ok, babe. Sasha isn't there. She was released from Deveon when you found the black stone. She came through the portal into the compound before we summoned the gods.".

My eyes go round. "Before what?"

"Oh right, we got distracted," he tells me sheepishly. "Since you've been missing, Aliyah and Isaiah returned home. We confronted the Anhelios, thinking they had taken you and Kate. They hadn't, but we discovered that Lutheran is actually with us. He has been playing the other side for centuries, waiting for Aliyah's return ... and oddly for Keyra to reemerge. Apparently they were lovers before we became the Fallen ..."

"What?" I screech. "So Rafa isn't Kate's fated mate? Is it Lutheran?" I stare at my lover in shock and disgust. "I have to tell you, Az. Lutheran wasn't as bad as the other Anhelios, but he was an asshole. I would not wish him on my worst enemy as a mate." I try to shake off the bad feeling.

"I know, baby, but I really do believe most of that was an act to try to fit in with the other Anhelios."

I shake my head in disgust. "I guess we'll see who Kate chooses once we get her back.".

"True. Although Lutheran did help us summon the gods which was dangerous and tricky."

"Ok. About that ..." I say slightly confused "Why would you do that? Honestly I've met them, and I have to say, they are intimidating as fuck."

"You met them? When did they take you?"

"Yes, I met them. I give that shit zero stars. I do not recommend fucking with them. They were scary and incredibly condescending."

Azrael snorts. "Right, babe. Because they are literal gods. Gods are dicks. It's kinda in the job description. What did they say?"

"They were challenging me as the Deveon warrior. They said that I would have to complete a series of trials and tests in order to find you, and that once I did, we would need to complete the bonds in order to release my Deveon warrior. So I will have to complete our bonds and accept my true nature in order to return home, right?"

"Yes. Are you ok with that?"

I stare at him. "Um I appreciate you asking, but it isn't like we have a real choice here, right? I chose you before the gods took me, and I choose you now."

Azrael kisses me, and I smile at him "So, about the tunnel to get here ... it's not easy, and to be honest, I'm not sure you will fit. It was a tight fit for me to swim through, and you're, like, at least twice my size."

Azrael laughs, "Baby, we can just teleport. I'm a literal fucking demon."

I frown at him. "Wait. Sasha is a demon too, right? You said she helped you summon the gods?"

Azrael nods, "Yes."

"So she could have teleported me here? I didn't actually have to do the whole fucking quest thingy?"

Azrael laughs. "I think the quest was the point, babe. I don't think she could have just teleported you here and gotten the same results."

"Huh," I grumble. "I'm not sure I actually buy that," I say as he steps into his pants and buttons his shirt.

Azrael opens his arms and I walk into them. "Visualize the cave where you left Sasha with your clothes."

I do, and when I open my eyes, we are standing in the cave with the wall of amethyst and the emerald green pool of water. I smile and step into my booty shorts. I pull my sports bra over my head and am adjusting the band when someone clears their throat behind us.

"Lovely of you to join us, Nyx. Azrael. We can see that you have been getting reacquainted with one another," Enhil says as she looks at us with disgust.

Ishtar examines her nails and laughs. "Well, Azrael, you've become quite the dirty human, haven't you? Partaking in the pleasures of the flesh like a, well, animal. It's disturbing really." She turns her attention to us and frowns. "Disgusting."

Enki laughs. "It's fitting really. His desire for her has become his downfall." He smirks at us. "Go ahead. Ask me—what do I mean by that?" he taunts us.

I swallow hard and ask the question he is begging me to ask. "What do you mean, Enki?"

The three gods laugh. "It was a trap, Nyx. You fool. There was never really a Challenge. We couldn't care less if you completed the trials and tests," Enhil says with contempt.

"We just needed Azrael to be desperate enough to have you so that he would overlook how obvious it all was and come for you. You, my dear, were just the carrot we dangled to get the prize," Enhill says softly.

"You fell for it, you fools. You wanted to rut against one another so badly that you looked past an obvious trap and teleported yourself into Deveon. A dimension we created as a literal cage to imprison you, Azrael. Welcome home. This elaborate ruse was all for you," Ishtar says, clapping her hands.

I watch the sibling gods in horror. "Why Azrael?" I'm confused as to why they went to all this trouble to set me up and trap my lover.

Enhil turns her golden eyes on me and smiles a terrifying smile that contorts her beautiful features to a ghastly mask. "Whatever do you mean, child?" she asks with an air of innocence.

I step towards her, meeting her terrifying eyes with a direct stare. "Why do all of this to trap Azrael and not the others? Unless you mean to take us all one by one." My voice trails off as the realization hits me that this is a long game. The gods are attempting to pick us off and level the playing field so that the Anhelios can annihilate the human race.

I watch as Enhil reads the thoughts straight from my mind. Her smile widens, and her eyes glitter at my fear as true understanding of what is at stake flows through me.

Azrael grips my hand tightly and pushes images through our fated mates' bond. I watch in horror as he shows me images of Aliyah and the others meeting with the gods. The message is clear. The gods cannot lie, but the questions must be worded correctly. I squeeze his hand in response and turn my attention to the conversation at hand.

"Of course we wanted all of the Fallen. Unfortunately Aliyah and Isaiah have completed their bonds and escaped our plans for the moment. You and your friend Keyra are inconsequential while still in your human forms, but you do serve as bait for the other Fallen," Enhill tells me with a horrifying smirk as she gestures to Azrael.

I swallow down my fear and clench Azrael's hand as I attempt to hide my fear and rage at the inevitable loss of our lives and our one chance at saving humanity. I show Az images of us distracting the gods while we find a way to connect with the universal knowledge. He nods tightly.

Ishtar laughs, a crazed and disturbing sound. "Ah, how annoyingly hopeful of you, Nyx. It's amusing how you still believe you have a chance at, well, anything resembling escape." She laughs openly and turns to Azrael. "And you are a terrible disappointment. We had hoped to have a challenge here. We had hoped you would prove to be a better opponent, Azrael. And yet here you are, a lovesick fool who walked straight into our trap." She admonishes my mate, and I feel a cold numbness seeping in as I realize I have to ground and connect to the higher knowledge if we have any chance at escape.

Just as I think the thoughts, the gods hear them. Ishtar laughs, and Enki turns cold eyes in my direction. "You have been impressive, Nyx. If that helps to take the sting of our betrayal and your loss away."

He smiles at me, much as a friend would when comforting you. I see the lie in it before the smile falls from his face. "Even in human form, you have come much further than we could have anticipated. Not close enough. You have not completed your bonds. You are helpless to defend yourselves against us. Three bonds were all you accomplished before we stole you away. Pathetic really." He tisks in our direction.

I clear my mind and push the images of a blank slate towards my lover. So far, the gods don't seem to be able to read our mates' bond. We have to remain calm and grounded.

I utilize the angelic bond to open my knowledge chakra. We are all connected. We have the power and ability to save ourselves. I know it in my heart. Utilizing the universal bond while Azrael interacts with the god siblings, I instinctively close down the telepathic bond, much as I did for Aliyah and Isaiah during their breakup. I can feel the peace wash over me as the gods are closed out of my thoughts.

I now know that they have no knowledge of the bonds we've completed since coming to Deveon. They don't know what happens in different realms. They can't read our thoughts when we are connected to universal knowledge.

I smile and turn to Azrael, but he doesn't appear to be able to read my thoughts either. Interesting. I focus on opening my sixth chakra and let the power of knowledge flow through me.

The immense power is overwhelming and I barely hold my stance as the information flows into me at breathtaking speeds. It is painful to absorb the knowledge while in human form, but I hold still and filter through it until the understanding that I must utilize the power of sacrifice to save us stands out to me.

They don't know we have only one bond left.

They don't know it is the sacrifice bond. They can't deny a true sacrifice when offered.

I now understand I must sacrifice myself in order to complete our bonds. In order to give Azrael the power of my Deveon warrior.

It will most likely kill me. I see that now. If not, I will be caged here in hell for gods only know how long. It doesn't matter if we can complete the bonds; it may give the other Fallen a chance at completing our destiny. It is the only option.

I close the chakra and with it, the flow of information. I take a deep breath and mentally prepare for what is to come.

I shake off the fear as rage washes through me and with it, more power than I had ever thought possible.

I step forward. "No. Fuck no. I won't allow any of it. I sacrifice myself. You cannot have him. Open the portal, Azrael. Go home. They cannot deny a true sacrifice made in their name.".

My anger is palpable. Electricity zaps along my body and throughout the air around us. Thunder claps in the distance, and I feel our sixth bond snap into place. It feels stronger than the others, and the finality of it takes my breath away. I feel all the memories, emotions, and power as it flows into me. The intensity of the bond is overwhelming, and as I collapse to the ground, I can hear Ishtar screaming in anger at my defiance. I don't care. The darkness takes me with a smile on my face.

Chapter Twenty-One

Sacrifice

Azrael

Chaos ensues as Nikki denies the gods' claim to me and stakes her own by sacrificing herself in my place and completing the final bond.

I watch in horror as she crumbles to the floor before me. Ishtar screams at Nikki for defying the gods, and Enki and Enhil exchange looks as my whole world comes to a screeching halt. My lover, my mate, and the woman to whom I have sworn eternity is in a heap on the floor of the cave.

I move to her in what feels like slow motion. When I finally reach her, it feels like crashing into a protective wall of energy. Something powerful protects my mate as she convulses on the floor. I cannot get to her, and the helplessness is overwhelming.

Nikki screams in agony. Her screams mingle with Ishtar's as they compete for the more tortured soul. I hope with all my heart that Ishtar wins this battle of extremes.

I watch in horror as Nikki seems to be burning, the blue electricity from our fifth bond is back but in extremes. It runs along her body, scorching all her nerve endings as she convulses. She screams until her voice is raw and hoarse. I push against the invisible wall of energy surrounding her but cannot get to her.

Nikki raises from the ground to a crouched position. Her screams have stopped, but she clutches her head in what appears to be agony.

Moments pass, but it feels like an eternity. And then she stands tall and drops her arms to her side as she cracks her neck and a terrifying smile crosses her lips. She holds out her hands, and the fire that cracked along her skin is now a glowing orb of purple energy.

Knowledge. Nyx's super power is some type of knowledge and the ability to weaponize this knowledge.

I smile with her as she moves this orb of vibrant energy from hand to hand. She looks at the gods as they stand before her, and she laughs. Huge black and gold wings erupt from her back and float in the air around her, making her appear larger than life. Beautiful, twisted black bone horns sprout from her forehead, and I have never seen her more beautiful. Her skin glows with the new life force and energy of immortality.

"Who are the fools now?" she asks the gods, and they stare at her without reaction. "You said I was back in the game when you decided to challenge me. I wasn't then, but trust me when I say, I am back now. And I believe I just out maneuvered the three of you," she announces boldly.

Enki begins a slow mocking clap, and Nyx turns her head to look at him in a way more terrifying than any god. Her power glows and emanates from her.

He slowly drops his hands "Well played, Nyx. You have earned your place in the hierarchy of immortality. Just remember who rules this domain and tread carefully."

Enhill nods at Nyx in acknowledgement. "You have done well in recognizing our weaknesses and using them against us. You are a true warrior. While this Challenge was a hoax to enslave Azrael, you have excelled in using our own game against us. I am impressed that you were able to see through our power and find our need for sacrifice in order to use it to win this round," she says in a tone of boredom.

Ishtar steps forward. "You may have won this round, Nyx, but you will not win the game. We did not see this coming. And yet there is much more to come. Two down ... two to go," she says with a mocking laugh and then the gods are gone as quickly as they appeared.

"Nyx." I breathe out when the gods have gone, and we are alone. She turns to me and smiles brighter than I have seen her smile before.

"Azrael. My lover. My mate. I was so terrified when they claimed you as a prisoner. And then I was more angry than I have ever been in this lifetime or before. How dare they try to take you from me again."

She moves to me, and I slide my arms around her waist and lift her so that her legs close around my waist and her arms slide around my neck. Her wings flutter around us, and I close mine, dropping them to lie against my back as her wings enclose me and hold me to her. I gently stroke her horns and kiss the skin they sprouted from.

"Are we truly free, Az? Did we do it?" she asks, bewildered that the sacrifice worked and her true form was claimed.

I smile at her. "You did it, baby. We're free."

"Is this what you had hoped for, Azrael? Am I her to you? Or is too much of Nikki still ingrained in me?"

I stare at her in confusion. "How do you feel, Nyx? Are you, well, you?"

Nyx smiles at me and laughs with ease. "I'm me. I feel strong and powerful. I wield a powerful sense of self, as well as a knowledge I've never had before. Bonding brings new strength and unimaginable power. But I'm still Nikki too. I'm still angry and resentful and hardened by a life that was unfair and yet made me, well, me. I still want you with a desire that borders on pain, and I still want to save the damn world," she says with a truthfulness that rings pure in her words.

"You are amazing, my lover. You are powerful and strong. Terrifying and beautiful to behold. You sent the gods away with a newfound fear and respect for the Deveons, and I am beyond proud to be your man."

I find her lips with mine, and I kiss her with everything I have. All the passion, all the fear, all the helplessness and eventual happiness. I kiss her like I've never kissed any being before, and she clings to me.

"I love you, Nyx. I love you beyond reason. Beyond expectation. I will adore you and stand at your back as your guard and protector while you shine as the warrior you were always meant to be."

Nyx smiles at me with adoration, and I shine under her love. "You are mine, Azrael, and I am yours." She speaks the Oath of the Bonded with pride and love.

My Warrior has returned. She is powerful and strong with a sense of self that is refreshing. She was reborn of fire and brimstone. Of passion and sacrifice. And she is everything I could have prayed to the gods to bring back to me. She is the Deveon Warrior, and she has claimed me as her fated mate.

Chapter Twenty-Two

H onesty
Nyx

"So, you want to blow this popsicle stand or what?" I ask my lover while I am still in his arms. My Deveon wings encircle us and hold the man I adore close to me.

Azrael laughs and smiles down at me. "Are you done with this gilded cage so soon, my love? The guys and I spent a dozen centuries trapped in here, and you've only been here a fortnight," he teases, and I punch him in the arm playfully.

Azrael winces. "Careful, love, your increase in power has made you wicked strong."

I laugh until I see how red his arm is. That is definitely going to bruise. "Wow. I'm truly sorry, Az. I had no idea. But damn, look at me! I really am a superhero." I sing as I release my lover and do a little strut around him.

Azrael laughs at my antics. "Demon, you're a super demon."

I smile. "It's going to take a bit to get used to."

"I know. All of this was a lot. We did it though, baby. And now we just need to get back to humanity. Take a long soak in the tub and sleep for a week." He pulls me close for another sweet kiss.

I smile at my man. "I'm not going to lie. The Challenge was hard. Being stolen from my home, forced to find my way out of a hell dimension without the help of my lover or my people, and then ultimately hearing that I was played by three sibling gods who wanted to snatch my man and imprison him in a hell dimension kinda pissed me off."

Azrael stokes my wings, my hair, my back. "Yes. I am so sorry, Nyx. None of this was right or even remotely fair, and yet we succeeded. And being the one they fooled and walking into their trap, I would still do it all over again to get to you." He kisses my forehead and then my lips and along my jaw. "How did you know the sacrifice would work?" His voice is soft, his lips tracing mine.

I sigh as I melt into him. "While you were distracting the gods, I closed the telepathic bond and forced them out of my thoughts. Then I connected to the universal bond. Luckily for me, Gabriel had invaded my dreams and memories while I was in the amethyst cave. He pounded the concept of sacrifice and the gods' obsession with the rules surrounding said sacrifice into my human skull."

Azrael is still in my arms. "That is extremely impressive, love. You shouldn't have been able to access the universal bond in human form. Your powers are strong."

I smile with pride. "I can't take all the credit, Sasha helped me to learn and access the bond, and Gabriel was incredibly insistant in his concept of sacrifice."

Azrael's eyes darken. "Gabriel visited you in the cave?" His voice strains in an attempt to stay calm.

I nod as I run my hands along his back and under his shirt, seeking to comfort him. "He did. First a series of awful memories, in which we were friends and he tried to recruit me to their side. And then again in a dream-walk. Clearly he and Michael are still healing if he needs to dream-walk to get to me." I attempt to make the situation less upsetting to Azrael.

"Why did he tell you about the sacrifice?"

"He wasn't actually trying to help me with his warnings but rather terrify me in my human form to believe I was intended to be his sacrifice someday. He told me of the gods' obsession with sacrifice during his recruitment speech to scare me, and then he alluded to Sasha being his sacrifice when he killed her in front of me during the War of the Winged Beasts."

Both of us are still. My hands are no longer stroking his body, and his hands are placed on my waist. I swallow hard and continue. "I owe my powers of observation and the ability to think on my toes for the actual saving of you and me.".

Azrael smiles softly at me. "So you don't have some twisted gratitude towards that psycho? Or a misconstrued sense of obligation?" he asks me seriously.

I laugh a little bitterly. "Do I owe him for saving me and my man? Probably. Am I going to repay the favor someday? It's doubtful. He's still an evil and despicable being who literally has no soul."

I reach for Azrael's face and hold his head between my hands. "Speaking of my mate … I love you. I am beyond grateful to have found you and to have completed our bonds. I can't imagine any other soul that I could spend an eternity with but you, Azrael? Yes, please."

My lips find his. His kiss is deeper, more demanding this time, and I am desperate for his touch. I cling to him as his tongue traces the seam of my lips, demanding entrance. I open for him, and the taste of him is delicious.

"I love you, Nyx. I am so grateful to have found you. I am grateful to you for saving me from an eternity enslaved to the gods and for completing our bonds so that I get to hold you, kiss you, and fuck you for the rest of eternity."

His hands stroke over my face and neck, and he squeezes the base of my throat tightly.

My core tightens at the possessive touch. I press my breasts against his chest, my nipples tightening as lust runs through my veins. My core flutters as I press closer, and Azrael tightens his hold on my throat. A groan escapes me as I rub my thighs together. I wet my lips and bit his ear.

"Good gods, you are sexy and loyal and loving," I whisper as my tongue darts out to lick the crest of his ear. He shudders, and I smile. "Are you going to eventually convince me that I am worthy of love, Azrael?" I ask him as I shamelessly rub myself against his thigh, desperate for the friction.

Azrael groans and strokes his hand up my throat. I lean my head back, allowing him better access, and he squeezes at the top, his knuckles grazing my jaw.

"I hope so, baby. I'm going to spend every second I can showing you that you are loved and desired and worthy of every single orgasm I ring out of your sweet pussy."

This time I shudder. My pussy clenches at his words, and I can feel the ache beginning to form in my core.

"I want to ride your thick, hard cock, Az. I want the length of you pressed against my wetness until I can't stand it anymore, and I have to slam my hips down to get as much of you inside my cunt as possible."

Azrael laughs and reaches his hand down to cup my pussy. "Greedy, little cunt. Don't worry Nyx, I'll take care of your needs, baby." He slaps my pussy, and I clench harder.

It's at this exact moment that I know I am obsessed with this fallen angel, this demon. I snap my sharp teeth at my mate. "I'm going to spend an eternity loving you, Azrael. Even if you stop loving me, I'll love you enough for the both of us."

Azrael grips my pussy with one hand and my throat with his other as his wings close around me and gently lift me off the ground. He walks me to the closest wall as my legs close around his waist, and I rub my wet pussy against the hard length of his very substantial cock.

"You say the prettiest things, Nyx."

He strips my clothing from me and slams into me hard, his soft wings breaking the impact with the rough wall. I ride him like that. Hard and rough and then soft and sweet.

His lips close around my nipple, and his thumb works my clit until I'm crying out his name, and it echoes off the stone walls of this cave in hell. And I love it. I love the rough sex and the soreness I'm sure to feel for days after. I love that he has more than likely left bruises on my pale skin, and I know he bares my teeth marks and nail scratches. I love all of it.

Yep. I know, I know. My damage is showing. It happens sometimes. I'm not perfect. Even as a demon, I have my faults. I'm angry and vengeful. A little careless and definitely prone to pissing off the gods. I suppose you could call me a handful. That's ok. I've always been a little too much for most people. It's a damn good thing the Deveons aren't like most people.

And when it comes right down to it, Azrael likes my damage, and I definitely like his. We are a match made in heaven and eventually again in hell.

· · · ·

Azrael and I are dressing a little while later. We are quiet now. Little touches here and there but mostly just coming down from all the craziness of our confrontation with the gods and our final bonds.

I smile over at my mate. He smiles back and wraps his arms around me. "Are you ready to go home Nyx?"

"Yes, please. I am excited to get back to the compound and relax a bit before we have to figure out what to do about the Anhelios."

"Understood. That sounds nice. Maybe a little staycation. I can cook and wait on you while you relax and unwind?" he says teasingly.

I laugh and snuggle into his arms. "Yes, please. And then we can sort out our people. I can't wait to see Aliyah and Isaiah, and Rafa and Ka." My words trail off as I remember that Kate is still missing.

I turn to Azrael with widened eyes. "Oh shit, Kate! Where the hell is she, Az? We have to find her. What if the gods sent her here, and we don't know how to find her?"

Azrael squeezes me a little tighter to him. My chin fits against his chest as he strokes my hair. "She isn't here, Nyx. When we summoned the gods back in the human realm, they said some riddle about her being right in front of us and yet nowhere at all at the same time."

"What the fuck is that supposed to mean?" I'm suddenly angry again with the gods on my friend's behalf. Azrael holds me tighter and drops a kiss on the top of my head.

"I honestly don't know, baby. We'll figure it out though. I didn't have time to discuss with the others what the gods could have meant since our bond clicked into place and I was brought here to help you."

"To be saved by me, you mean," I grumble, and Azrael laughs.

"Right, that was exactly what I meant to say."

I laugh with him.

"Ok, so Kate is still missing and the gods are teasing us that she is still in the human realm ... just not?" I try to work the possibilities around in my head.

"Right. They also said that Sasha is somehow the key to finding her or something along those lines."

"So, then, maybe Sasha brought her back by now?" I ask hopefully.

Azrael looks doubtful. "It's possible. I suppose. But Sasha didn't remember anything. She had some type of amnesia when she stepped through the portal."

"Wait, what?"

"Supposedly Sasha has the ability to locate her if Sasha could remember who Sasha actually is. She's had a bit of memory loss since passing over into the human world after so many centuries in a hell dimension."

"Good gods." I groan, frustrated "We seriously cannot catch a fucking break with those dicks. It's like they outmaneuver us every damn time."

Azrael's eyes grow warm as he smiles down at me, "Well, not every time."

"Right. We did good. We can do this." I feel slightly bolstered at the memory that we did outsmart the gods. I completed my challenges and found a way to complete the bonds with Azrael despite everything they threw in our way.

"Ok, babe. Let's do this. Let's go home and help Sasha remember who she is, find Kate, and finish off the Anhelios before the gods can throw any more wrenches into the plan." I am determined to annihilate the threat to humanity now that I've unleashed my Deveon Warrior.

Azrael smiles as he closes his eyes. He conjures a golden ball of energy in the space before us. Opening his eyes, he smiles at me, "Ready?"

I nod and reach for his hand as the portal opens, and we step through.

I wish we had known what we were coming home to. Maybe we would have been more prepared. Maybe we could have done something different. I don't know. I suppose it doesn't matter now. Honestly I never could have envisioned the hell we were about to step into after walking out of a literal hell dimension. Life is fucked up like that sometimes.

Chapter Twenty-Three

Homecoming
      Nyx

Nothing is the same. For me it's been a few days, maybe a week. For them, months. Literal months of fighting for their lives, for the lives of every human being on earth.

Our people have been desperately trying to hold off an apocalypse. All while we were making love and playing games with gods. My anger implodes at the unfairness of our reality at times.

. . . .

Azrael and I stepped through the portal and into what had been the living area of the Deveon compound. Now it was some type of command center. We had expected to come home to deal with the Anhelios and potentially more of the gods' interference; instead we stepped into the middle of what appeared to be an apocalypse.

"Thank the gods, you're both safe," Aliyah says as we step into what is apparently their main command center. She quickly steps forward to hug me and then Azrael. "Nyx, you look amazing!" Aliyah tells me as she looks me over. "Look at those wings, girl. Gorgeous. I knew you and Az had completed the bonds since we felt the increase in power when you did." She gives me a secretive smile.

I nod to my friend in acknowledgement and notice that as beautiful as she is, she looks hardened. Her face has lost much of its innocence, and she is bruised with more scars than I remember. "Thank you, Aliyah." I tell her as Azrael squeezes my arm in comfort.

"Congratulations to both of you. Aliyah and I are truly happy for you." Isaiah comes up behind Aliyah and wraps his arms around her waist. "The power increase in your bond was phenomenal. No wonder the Anhelios were so intent on keeping us all apart."

"Unfortunately the Anhelios felt it too, and with Michael and Gabriel back around the same time as your bonds, all hell broke loose here, literally," Aliyah continues. "I wish we had more time to discuss your bond. I'd love to hear about your experiences.".

I smile at my friend. "Another time, my Queen. Tell us what's happening. It looks like a damn apocalypse.".

"You're not wrong. I am truly thankful you're back. I need my fiercest warrior and my general. We'll fill you in on the situation here." She gestures to the room around her.

There are humans and archangels spread throughout the compound. I look over Aliyah's shoulder to see movement in the atrium behind her. There are twenty or so soldiers training next to the pool area.

"After Michael and Gabriel returned, they released some type of pathogens into the air on earth. It is slowly killing the humans and making the archangels sick. Lutheran left the Anhelios shortly before they attacked and informed us of their intentions. We were able to recruit as many archangels and humans as possible."

Looking around the room we are standing in, there are ten or eleven soldiers utilizing the whiteboards to discuss potential attack strategies, and I imagine it is like this or similar in every room of the house. I turn to Aliyah with wide eyes just as Azrael steps closer to me. His wings snap out, and it takes substantial will power for him to reign in his emotions and settle his large wings against his back. Only a few people seem to notice, and they quickly return to whatever they were doing before our intrusion.

"Gods, Aliyah. What the hell has happened?" Azrael asks in shock.

"Chaos, Az. After you left, Lutheran and I got to work recruiting humans and archangels alike. Lutheran filled us in on the Anhelios' plan for the Apocalypse, and we knew immediately that we would have to grow our army tenfold before Michael and Gabriel returned. Luckily Lutheran has been working tirelessly over the past millennium, convincing his followers to be our followers." She stops and smiles fondly at her friend. "Honestly I don't know where we would be without him. After the Anhelios released the toxins, the humans and archangels were forced underground. We have offered shelter to as many as possible."

"So you have hundreds, if not thousands, in the catacombs underground?" Azrael asks, and I look at them both in shock.

Aliyah nods. "Yes. They are training and keeping away from the literal outdoors until the pathogens fade."

Az nods as if he expected as much. "How long do we think until the toxins are gone from the air?".

Isaiah shrugs. "At least several more weeks, if not months, until it is safe for the humans. For now, we are forced to keep them here and underground. They are adjusting better than expected, but it is still a difficult situation."

"Gods. What a damn mess," I say softly. "I'm so sorry I wasn't here for all of this."

Aliyah reaches for me and squeezes my shoulders. "It isn't your fault, Nyx. The gods stole you away. It was necessary for you and Azrael to do what was needed. And," she says, smiling tightly as she releases me, "you are both back now and better than ever."

"Things have been hard for everyone, but Lutheran has been great, and Sasha has been a literal godsend since her return." Aliyah gestures to the woman in question who is currently reviewing strategies with several other soldiers a few feet away. "I am beyond thankful to have my best warrior and general back in this realm." She embraces me again, and Isaiah comes from behind to slap Azrael on the back.

"The bonds look good on you, Az. You both look truly happy," Isaiah tells my mate, and I smile at the compliment. Azrael squeezes my fingers as he and Isaiah move away.

"Being bonded to Nyx is the best thing I can imagine. The shared powers and abilities should be helpful in dealing with all of this," I hear him say as they move away.

"So Lutheran is with us now?" I ask my Aliyah, circling around to her earlier statement.

"Yes. He has been incredibly helpful. We have been hopeful that you and Az would find your way back to us, as well as Keyra, but there have been several attacks and battles since the Anhelios have their leader back. Things have been difficult here, and without you and Azrael, Lutheran and Sasha have been amazing."

"I'm glad. Sasha was a good friend to me in Deveon. She was immensely helpful, and I am grateful for her friendship, even when I didn't know her. After the bonds, of course, my memories were returned, and I remember her from our lifetime before we were Fallen. Although, apparently as a demon, she could have teleported me to the amethyst caves ... and she didn't, so she definitely has some explaining to do there," I joke to Aliyah.

She smiles sadly. "Sasha has been wonderful, but unfortunately while she recognizes that we are familiar to her, she doesn't actually have any memories of any of us."

I shake my head. "A parting gift from the gods?"

"Possibly. The gods are well known for being vengeful and petty. Perhaps they stole her memories when they released her from Deveon. We had hoped, in time, they would return, but now I believe only a true bonding will bring them back."

"Is that a possibility?"

"Yes. Rafa and Sasha have the pull of the bond. We believe they are fated mates," she tells me quietly. I stare at her in shock.

"But Kate and Rafa ..." My words trail off. I put my hand over my mouth "Does that mean Kate is dead?"

"No," Aliyah says confidently. "No. I don't think Kate is dead. I believe that Kate and Lutheran may be fated mates."

My eyes shoot over to the Anhelio that held us captive for so many months in the dungeon of their compound. A shiver slides down my spine at the thought that my friend may be destined for someone like that. I stare at Aliyah in horror.

She shakes her head. I look back to Lutheran and catch him watching us. "It is for the two of them to decide once we find her," Aliyah says.

I swallow hard and nod to my queen. "Speaking of Kate, is there any word on her whereabouts?" I'm concerned that she has been missing for no less than three, maybe four, months now.

Aliyah shakes her head sadly. "No. Nothing. The last we heard was when the gods gave us some type of riddle concerning her when we summoned them to find you both."

"Yes, Azrael mentioned this. He said they said something to the effect of, *she was right in front of us and yet nowhere at all.*".

"Yes. I don't know what it means though."

I look back over to Sasha and Lutheran, and they are both watching us intently. Sasha makes her way over to us.

"I couldn't help but overhear ... did you say you believe Kate is dead?"

Aliyah shakes her head. "No. I don't believe so. I think I would feel the connection between us severed, and I don't. I just can't feel her or hear her, but I have this tingling sensation where she should be, if that makes any sense."

Sasha nods. "Actually it does make sense. What if what the gods meant that Kate, or Keyra, was non-corporal?" she asks, working out some type of theory as she speaks.

Aliyah looks as confused as I feel. "Non-corporal? Like a ghost?"

Sasha nods excitedly. "Yes, exactly like a ghost. What if the gods stole her physical form but left her here to haunt the Deveons without the ability to communicate?"

I stare at Sasha horrified. "You mean she could be here, right now, desperate to communicate with us and unable to do so?"

Sasha nods. "Yes. But didn't the gods say I was the key to finding Keyra?" She turns to Aliyah.

Aliyah nods to Sasha. "Yes, they did say that, but how can you find her when you can't remember who you are?"

Sasha smiles at our queen tightly. "Well, then I better figure out who I am and what my powers have to do with our missing friend before this apocalypse thing gets even more out of control," she tells us with a confidence I am far from feeling.

I watch Sasha thoughtfully as she returns to her place next to Lutheran. Gods, help us. I'm not sure where Kate is or if she can be reached if she is non-corporal, but I am suddenly very invested in Rafa and Sasha completing their bonds in order to get my best friend back from whatever hell the gods have stuck her in. Keyra was our healer, and something tells me that it wasn't an accident they stole her before the Anhelios unleashed a toxin unlike any the world has ever seen.

About the Author

Jennifer Marcia is a writer, reader, and lover of books. She exists primarily on very strong coffee and snuggles from her lovable rescue dogs while she gives voice to the characters in her imagination. She believes in strong, capable, and often emotionally damaged heroines who can save themselves, heroes who are dangerous and incredibly sexy, and who treat their women with all the love and respect. Her supporting characters are well-rounded and fierce because we're all simply drifting through life without a strong system of love and support from our people.

Jennifer lives in Northern California on a farm with her own HEA, her pups, and a flock of chickens. She hopes to be able to continue to write and farm and snuggle her man without interruption for as long as possible.

Read More from Jennifer Marcia

<u>jennifermarciaauthor | Instagram, Facebook, TikTok | Linktree</u>[1]

---

1. https://linktr.ee/jennifermarciaauthor

Please Remember To Leave A Review

Thank you for reading this novel. I am blessed to be able to do what I love in life. If you enjoyed it, pop over to my Amazon[2], Bookbub[3] or Goodreads[4] Author Page and leave me a review. Your reviews help other readers decide if this is a novel they might enjoy. Help me spread the word, and allow me to continue writing. I wouldn't be able to do this without you, the reader. I appreciate you and am honored that you took the time to delve into this world with me. Thank you for your continued support.

XOXO ◈

Jennifer Marcia

---

2.   https://www.amazon.com/Challenging-Deveon-Warrior-Anheilos-Anhelios-ebook/dp/ B0CR5R6T2F

3.   https://www.bookbub.com/books/challenging-the-deveon-warrior-a-deveon-anheilos- saga-a-deveons-anhelios-saga-book-2-by-jennifer-marcia

4.   https://www.goodreads.com/book/show/204480605-challenging-the-deveon-warrior

Acknowledgement

Thank you to my readers. Without you, there would be no point in delving into this world and going on these crazy adventures. I appreciate you more than I can ever say. Your continued support of my writing is so appreciated. To my fantastic editor and beta reader Allison Hedon, this book would not be what it is without you. I am so grateful for your thoughts and support. To my amazing ARC Readers, thank you for taking a chance on this author and reading and reviewing Challenging the Deveon Warrior. Your help has been fantastic and I appreciate you so much. And to my own Happily Ever After, I love you, babe. Thank you for supporting this crazy dream of mine. For making dinner and coffee, doing the dishes while I'm caught up in this world, creating new adventures, and helping my characters find their own happily ever afters. I am so grateful to you. I'm happy we get to choose each other every day.

Praise For Author

Honor and Luca's love story is firey, magnetic, and against the odds. And that's why it's also intoxicating and hotter than hot. Danger and loss are part of their everyday world, but so is the rock-solid support of the MC brotherhood.

As their growing bond is threatened by a predator closing in, Honor becomes part of Luca's world in a way that will change it for good—highly recommended for readers who crave dark and steamy love stories with high stakes and unbreakable bonds.

I can't wait for book #2! .....Goodreads Reviewer

An exciting new voice in MC romance, and I look forward to reading more from this author. -Goodreads Reviewer

Really enjoyed the different characters and the storyline of such strong women who aren't afraid of taking their lives back. Looking forward to future stories of the alpha men of the MC and the women they will come to love and protect.- Amazon Reviewer

• • • •

Luca: A Brotherhood MC Novel 5.0 out of 5 stars
Sexy and thrilling
Reviewed in the United States on February 26, 2023
I read it as a standalone and loved it. The dance between Donnie and Aurora was full of fun tension and very steamy, and the plot was a page-turner. The motorcycle club angle was new for me, and I enjoyed that edgy side of life. I totally dug Donnie-Amazon Reviewer
- Donnie: A Brotherhood MC Novel
I can only review Awakening The Queen Of The Damned by Jennifer Marcia as I received it as an ARC.My first read of the author and I love the story; loads of smut, tension, and fated mates yet an aspect of enemies to lovers.. What's not to love...
Paranormal / Fantasy is another + in my books.

Want to read more, and excited to see where this story is going.-Goodreads Reviewer

- Awakening: The Queen of the Damned

Deveons & Anhelios Saga

• • • •

Humanity is about to perish.

Demons and Angels walk among us, and while we are taught to worship the Angels of human mythology, it is actually the Demons or Deveons that will be our saviors.

In a world on the verge of an apocalypse, three Deveon warriors must find their mates in human form, convince them that not only do Angels and Demons exist but that they are Deveon warriors banished to human form and the true fated mates of the Fallen 3.

The Deveons must bond and reveal their true forms before humanity is snuffed out by the very beings humans were taught to worship.

Awakening: The Queen of the Damned Book One

Aliyah Devon had never felt quite right. There had always been a voice in her dreams whispering for her to "wake up." For the past twenty-six years, she had felt like a dream walker in her own life until suddenly he appeared, and the world seemed to crash into blinding color and scorching heat.

Isaiah Donovan had been searching for his destined mate since she perished in war thousands of years ago. She was the leader of their people and the most powerful being of them all. Now she is fated to be a hunter trapped in human form until their bond can release her.

The human world is perishing, and Isaiah must find her and convince her that not only do Angels and Demons exist, and she is quite literally the queen of the damned, but that they are fated mates. She must bond with him and shed her human form before humanity is snuffed out by the very beings humans are taught to worship.

• • • •

C W/TW
Awakening is a suspenseful dark paranormal romance with dark themes. Please check your content and trigger warnings to make sure you are comfortable with the content:

18+ for on page sexual content, bondage, BDSM aspects, language, violence, some gore, and religious concepts.

• • • •

Challenging: The Deveon Warrior
Book Two

With humanity on the brink of an apocalypse, there is literally no time to spare. The Deveons, six fallen angels destined to save mankind, must fight the Anhelios and the Gods themselves to save not only one another and the whole of humanity but their fated mates.

People have always found Nikki St. James a little too much to handle. She is loud, opinionated, and feisty. She is also a chosen one. A human hunter destined to fight the Anhelios to help save humanity. She may also be one of the Fallen, A Deveon warrior forced to reincarnate in human form after trying to save humanity. If she is, she could very well be Azreal Dennison's true mate.

Azreal has spent millennia following his chosen brothers in their quest for the Deveon Queen. Now that they have found her, his own mate may be within arm's length until the gods rip her from this dimension in a twisted chess game to see who has the skills necessary to complete their bonds.

CW/TW

Challenging is a suspenseful dark paranormal romance with dark themes. Please check your content and trigger warnings to make sure you are comfortable with the content:

18+ for on page sexual content, bondage, BDSM aspects, language, violence, some gore, and religious concepts.

Embracing: The Deveon Empath
Book Three

With the Deveon and Anhelio war coming to a head and the end of humanity swinging in the balance, Sasha Delong is suddenly released from a hell dimension and thrown back into the battle between good and evil. Now she must embrace her true calling and step into the woman she was always meant to be. The only problem is she doesn't remember who that woman is. Can a bond with her fated mate bring back her memories and with it her knowledge of her own powers?

Rafael Donavon has always been hesitant about embracing the bonds and being tied to one woman for eternity, all of that changes when Sasha walks back into his life. Now Rafa wants to stay close and catch her if she slips on her rise to becoming the powerful empath the Fallen need her to be to defeat their enemies, but will she allow it or will she deny him the fated mate he believes her to be?

CW/TW

Embracing is a suspenseful dark paranormal romance with dark themes. Please check your content and trigger warnings to make sure you are comfortable with the content:

18+ for on page sexual content, bondage, BDSM aspects, language, violence, some gore, and religious concepts.

Coming Fall of 2024

• • • •

More Books By This Author

Luca: A Brotherhood MC Novel
Book One

• • • •

Luca Undertaker Stone isn't looking for love. He already had his love of a lifetime and lost her a decade ago. Now his darkness keeps women at a distance. He likes it like that. Running a self-defense and cage fighter training gym keeps him busy. Well, that and his side job as a contract killer. Soft and sweet has no place in his world.

That's good because Honor Williams is anything but soft and sweet. She's a verifiable badass who put a violent sexual predator back behind bars. Ok so maybe he's out now and stalking her. Maybe she's on the run. And maybe she's not quite so much a verifiable badass as she is telling herself she's one until she believes it. She doesn't date criminals and she sure as hell doesn't date sexy badass ex military contract killers.

They have no business hooking up. Honor needs to lay low and steer clear of trouble. Luca never dates and certainly doesn't sleep with a woman more than once. Honor just needs to learn self defense so she doesn't end up dead. Luca just wants to help her stay alive. It's not like they're going to fall in love.

• • • •

CW/TW
Luca is a suspenseful romance with dark themes. Please check your content and trigger warnings to make sure you are comfortable with the content:

18+ for sexual content, language, and violence.

Donnie: A Brotherhood MC Novel

Book Two

Donnie Lowe never stopped loving the first woman to own his heart. She was his secret lover ten years ago. At the time, he wanted to protect her. She was young and innocent with her whole life ahead of her. He was the President of a gun-running MC. He didn't have a right to corrupt her, but he'd done it anyway.

Aurora Dewitt isn't the same woman she'd been a decade ago when she asked her lover to kill the man who had murdered her little sister. Having left the only man who had ever really owned her heart because he didn't want her in his world, she clawed her way to the top of her own criminal enterprise. Aurora didn't need a man to do her dirty work now.

They had every intention of leaving the past where it belonged. They didn't know working together to stop the Cartel would bring back so many memories. It was only supposed to be a way to release stress; neither of them wanted to relive the rejection of their past together. How could they know they'd never stopped loving each other?

CW/TW

Donnie is a suspenseful romance with dark themes. Please check your content and trigger warnings to make sure you are comfortable with the content:

18+ for sexual content, language, and violence.

• • • •

Joe: A Brotherhood MC Novel
Book Three

Joe Reynolds has a protective streak a mile long, he is also incredibly loyal... perhaps to his own detriment. Joe is happy as a member of the local MC and running a lucrative and classy pub in the mainstreet area of his small town. He is not looking for love, his one and only long term relationship was an absolute disaster and as a result he has sworn off anything longer than a night and more serious than a quick slip between the sheets, especially with a gorgeous, smart and highly talented woman who previously dated a club brother and potentially broke that brothers heart. Nope, not gonna happen. So why is it proving so damn difficult to stay away?

Ella Jones is trouble. She has a past with the Brotherhood MC and did date one of Joe's MC brothers. It just wasn't the tortured love affair that Joe thinks it was and until her ex is ready to come clean and let her go for good she can't tell Joe the truth. Unfortunately for them both, they can't seem to stay away from one another. This is a problem for the Brotherhood as they fight off a Cartel that circles ever closer, a rival Mc that is out for blood and a madman who has his sights set on Ella.

Ella knows that Joe is damaged, she can't seem to stop herself from being drawn to the one man she can never have. He makes her feel things she has never experienced before. Somehow, she is determined to make him hers and to save him and herself in the process.

. . . .

CW/TW
Joe is a suspenseful romance with dark themes. Please check your content and trigger warnings to make sure you are comfortable with the content:

18+ for sexual content, language, and violence.

. . . .

Coming Summer 2024

Don't miss out!

Visit the website below and you can sign up to receive emails whenever Jennifer Marcia publishes a new book. There's no charge and no obligation.

https://books2read.com/r/B-A-LDNAB-ZMIGD

BOOKS 2 READ

Connecting independent readers to independent writers.

* 9 7 9 8 2 2 4 6 5 7 3 6 0 *